FOXFIRE

ROWAN HILL

PRAISE FOR ROWAN HILL

"Rowan Hill's FOXFIRE combines all the best elements of a tense, well-paced thriller with compelling folklore and horror, all in the stark, deadly and glittering setting of the frozen north. I was pulled in from the first page, captivated by layered characters and dynamics drawn with Hill's keen eye for the human condition, and a mystery that kept unraveling in unexpected and intriguing ways. Studded with prose that enhances the atmosphere of isolation and a yearning for connection, FOXFIRE is a hell of an experience, from beginning to end."

— LAUREL HIGHTOWER, AUTHOR OF CROSSROADS AND BELOW

"An unpredictable, high octane blend of whodunnit mystery and macabre folk horror. This one will keep you on your toes!"

— TIM MCGREGOR, AUTHOR OF WASPS IN THE ICE CREAM AND LURE

"A master of striking wilderness horror, Rowan Hill has concocted a violent treat particularly for those who enjoy their twisty crime thrillers laced with folkloric monsters and absolute carnage. A beautiful, grisly beast of a novel."

— KENZIE JENNINGS, AUTHOR OF RECEPTION & RED STATION

FOXFIRE

ROWAN HILL

Ebook ISBN: 9798988635406

Paperback ISBN: 9798988635413

Cover image by Teemu Puukka

❀ Created with Vellum

TRIGGER WARNINGS

Lite Domestic and sexual violence. Animal Death. Lite Gore.

Dedicated to my loving and supportive husband.

AINO

Sun and warmth were memories not to return for two months, and a strange twilight now flooded the sky with murky ocean-grays. Aino sniffed the frigid air, using her wrist instead of her cold, bloody hand to wipe her nose. She couldn't recall when the sky wouldn't even lighten to this miserable palette.

Polar midnight.

Darkness, absolute.

A week? Less?

The hanging, hollow carcass spat sylphs of faint steam, blood occasionally dripping into the metallic washing tub like errant raindrops. Crimson stars speckled surrounding snow in a gruesome constellation and Aino returned to the skinned body. With its front legs strapped to the branch above, the reindeer calf's head hung backward at an unsettling angle, facing the ancient forest behind the lodge rather than the young woman inexpertly skinning and carving him for dinner.

Her hands trembled, freezing. Shit. She'd left this chore too late. Extracting his offals had wasted an hour, the stink making her dry heave until she was inoculated against his putrid scents. Mattias had claimed some males needed separating and left hurriedly in his panic, conveniently forgetting Aino hadn't even *petted* a reindeer in five years. Now she was suddenly in charge of butchering one?

Eight for dinner. A loin and a leg? But Americans were coming, so more likely. How much did Americans eat? Would they take everything till the table was bare? Aino's imagination ran with images of obese and garish Southerners stuffing their faces like obscene caricatures, and she smiled and chuckled. The forest was quiet, observing her laughs turn to heavy breathing as she toiled, taking away one of its children, hacking its meat and sinews. She only paused once to listen to the caterwaul of the huskies, loud and obnoxious. Their cries ricocheted through the trees from their kennel, a five-minute walk north on a cleared path. But they had eaten earlier and Aino ignored them, hacking through tough flesh until gravity finally tore a string of muscle and the entire back leg of the reindeer fell into her cupped arms and waiting plastic apron. The comforting but dissipating warmth of the recently alive reindeer radiated through her layers of clothing and reminded Aino that Lapland was beyond fucking cold when one reveled in the heat of dead meat.

She turned for the lodge, arms loaded with his flesh, and stopped short. The Australian guest, newly arrived an hour prior, was leaning against the porch railing ten meters away, a cigarette hanging precariously from her lips.

She motioned to her own face, grinning. "Got blood on ya chin, there."

"Oh." Aino wiped her face against her shoulder and mounted the steps. The slightly older woman, Carly, held the door open.

"I was just 'bout to use this outhouse, but you want me and Kurt to help and clean that up?" Carly motioned to the macabre hanging carcass and washtub full of blood and floating organs. Aino stopped and frowned at the murder scene. Carly explained, "You know, because of bears... foxes... wolves?"

Aino's brain lagged as she readjusted her grip on the reindeer's skinned and fleshy limb between them, and then she said all at once,

"Oh, shit. Yes. Ummm, please. Yes, can you drag that washtub to the shed and bring the knives inside? I'll get Mattias...my dad, to cut the carcass down and bring it in."

Carly nodded casually, curiously undisturbed by the gruesome work, even smiling with teeth too big for her mouth and Aino continued inside. The main room of the lodge, once her grandfather's, was hot. The fireplace of the recently renovated gathering room heated the large space sufficiently and she glanced at his painting above the fire as she stepped quickly across polished wood floors, careful of dripping blood. Aino entered the new kitchen and laid the leg across the prepping station. Her grandfather, an old grizzled woodsman, had muttered some wild things when she was a child, but she distinctly remembered something about cutting meat. Stripping *down* with the muscle. Something Aino certainly didn't learn at the University of Helsinki.

"They're here!" her father called from the front door.

"Okay?" she replied, raising the knife when he hollered insistently, alarm in his voice.

"Aino! We greet guests! It's a proper hotel thing!"

She exhaled, irritated, and stabbed the knife into the dismembered leg. Disrobing and hanging the apron, Aino quickly washed her hands of sticky blood and crossed the main room, winding around sets of tables and chairs, the merry and cozy Christmas tree with red and green flickering lights, and met Mattias at the door.

"Remember your English, yes? And big smiles—whatever they need, we help. Okay?" He clapped her shoulder and they stepped outside, his eyes drifting to her chin, and he extracted a handkerchief from his pocket.

"You have blood on your chin."

She took it, wiping as the sleek black van turned the corner of the long driveway, snow crunching beneath its weight. In the twilight, it didn't use headlights, and the driver's white, charming smile glowed against the dark interior like the Cheshire cat. The van stopped in front of the porch stairs and Mattias quickly descended, opening the rolling door in a flourish.

"Welcome, friends!" he fawned.

A loud, brash American voice bawled, and a striking man stepped out with a long and muscular leg hidden by jeans. "Woohee! This is hog-killing weather. Shit, it's cold!" He was all jaw and a wide smile displaying teeth all the way back to his molars. Aino didn't know whether to swoon or be horrified by seeing all his teeth at once. He wore appropriate winter clothes but topped them with an odd cowboy hat accentuating his square face. Straightening and stretching his limbs, he rose half a foot over her father, standing over two meters tall.

Mattias opened his palms and his apologetic tone annoyed his daughter, as if he could apologize for the Finnish Arctic being cold. "This is Northern Lapland, my friend. At Christmas."

"Right, right, of course, home of the ole Sant-ee Claus!" the American laughed, gripping Mattias' hand in his wide one. They shook too enthusiastically and the handsome bear of a man stepped aside for the other passengers, subtly glancing at Aino as he stretched, arching his back and shaking out his legs.

A Japanese man exited next. Although smaller, less stocky, less imposing, and his face passive in the way a rock might show emotion, he was the most intimidating man Aino had ever seen. It wasn't the all-black, austere winter fleeces, nor the way he simply nodded to her father instead of warmly shaking hands. It was the way he carried himself: Simply standing beside the van. Stiff. Beneath his thick layers, Aino sensed every muscle in his body remained tense, waiting for some unknown threat. He glanced aside, also nodding to her, and turned to the van, holding his taut hand out at chest height.

A slender and effete hand stretched and accepted it, pressing for an anchor, and a Japanese woman emerged from the van like a captive butterfly in a dark cocoon. Garbed in a long, cream coat with angular hems reminiscent of a Japanese robe, she was elegant and graceful, stepping to the ground on light, floaty feet. Aino unconsciously smiled, warmed by this woman's movements and character. The woman examined the darkening Northern sky and the picturesque wooden lodge hedged in by snow with wonder. Dimples puckered her fair skin when she grinned, and it was delightfully charming. If this pair were married, they were chalk and cheese.

They walked away and the last guest embodied everything Aino knew from American movies. Long platinum locks peeked from a white fluffy Ushanka hat, tendrils spiraling down an expensive matching snowsuit. Beauty-pageant beautiful, she wore flawless makeup, gaudy with purple eyeshadow and lips a similar shade of violet.

Ski bunny.

Aino bridled her smirk.

The Bunny used Mattias's hand. Smiling, she was a dentist's wet dream with teeth as neon and blinding as her outfit.

"Well bless me, this is just preeeecious! Rocky, babe! You seeing this?"

Aino nearly laughed aloud at her ridiculous accent. The woman alighted and held Mattias lightly by the shoulders, leaning in and kissing his cheeks like a European.

"Mattias, this is delightful, darlin'. But lord, it's so cold and dark! It's only two pee-em!"

Mattias chuckled and guided her up the stairs with one hand like he led a princess. His English was stiff and over-pronounced. "It is nice to see you again, Regina. We have fires and hot chocolate waiting inside. Please, please," he laughed again, superfluously, and the four guests scaled the porch stairs.

Aino nodded amicably, avoiding eye contact as they passed into the home, and was startled by a heavy thud beside her.

Wilholm, the young driver, fair and boyishly handsome, smirked and threw another bag her way. He wore only a fleece, accustomed to the extreme cold, as opposed to herself, who'd lived in Helsinki for the last decade. Aino leaned on the porch's post and openly watched the muscles of his bare hands flex as he laid down a long and heavy ski bag, her cheeks warming. When the last bag sat on the porch, he sauntered over, something Aino thought impossible in bulky clothing.

"You've been back for a month already. When are you going to let me take you out?"

"We went grocery shopping together last week."

He raised an arm above his head and leaned on her post, grinning as he stepped up to her, and Aino's body was all at once heavy and hollow.

"*You* were grocery shopping when I caught you in the cheeses like a mouse. I want a real date."

"You live an hour away and the nearest restaurant is two," she jested half-heartedly, and he stepped closer. His face turned serious, the smile lines from his cheeks gone, and he spoke low with a tone reminiscent of whispered secrets.

"Let me take you on the boat to the sea, maybe under the lights one night, yeah? Some wine, some music..." He leaned forward and his hot breath blew against her. He had chewed mint gum on the drive and Aino stared at his mouth, so close, flushed red from the cold. It hypnotized her for a too-long moment, and he leaned perilously close, invitingly.

Aino murmured, "That sounds like a very romantic date."

"Oh, it will be, Aino."

He drew down, comfortingly taller than her, those red lips parting and his minty breath mingled with hers.

"Very sexy, Wilholm."

"Oh, *very* sexy, Aino."

Aino's wrist flicked, quickly pushing him away and he backed down a stair. "It also sounds like a very good way to get stuck here. I told you, I don't know if I want to stay after helping Mattias set up this damn resort."

Wilholm retreated another step, pursing those plump red lips, squinting and studying her before turning and searching the surroundings of the lodge. Beyond the wide-open circle serving as a car U-turn, forest, wild and ancient, stretched in every direction besides the slender driveway leading to the main road a kilometer away. Wilholm's charming smile returned. He wasn't cross, rather amused, and wagged a cold finger at her. "You haven't been back here since you were twelve. I promise you, you'll fall in love with the forest again." He arched an eyebrow, "You'll fall in love with everything. I swear it." He whispered like they were co-conspirators.

"I am STILL waiting!" A cross voice hollered in thick Meänkieli, the local dialect, from inside the van's recesses. Aino's gaping mouth snapped shut.

"Who's that?"

"I'm coming!" Wilholm called to the remaining passenger and then spoke low. "Some old man approached me outside the landing strip while I was waiting for the American's plane. Calls himself Virtanen and says his house is another twenty minutes up the road, though I don't know of it. Do you know if your grandfather ever sold any of his land?"

Aino scoffed. "No, he would never sell anything. To *anyone*. If he lives on our land, it's not legal," she whispered and descended the steps quietly, leaning subtly forward to sneak a look at the passenger. In the guts of the van waited a figure more beast than man. Dressed in traditional furs, a bushel of black beard, salt and pepper, covered most of his face, and his wild blue eyes whipped to the inquisitive Aino, catching her. She leaned in, raising a hand in greeting,

"Hello, sir! I'm—"

"I know who you are, girl!" he gruffed, his accent thick and cloying on his lips like honey lived there. "Are you like your father or your grandfather?" He asked this quickly, as if he expected an answer just as fast.

"Oh, uh, neither? I guess?"

He grunted again, a beastly retort, and readjusted the bulk of his furs tighter. "Just as well. I was sorry when he passed." His eyes fell to his hands, bare and bony, years of hard living in the threads and wrinkles. "We were friends, of a kind." His hands squeezed into fists and his voice hardened again.

"You make sure to stay inside at night, yes? No place for city-folk! Don't need you and all those strangers getting lost and waking everyone up with your cries. Now tell that boy to come along now," he commanded.

Aino stepped out of his view, her eyebrows raised at the odd demand. Wilholm passed her, and they nudged shoulders together playfully as they once did as schoolmates, but then he took her naked hand and raised it to his mouth. He blew a heated breath over it and somehow it warmed her hollow belly.

"I'll be back in a few days for your guest. Stay warm, city mouse. You may be used to snow, but the cold here bites you like teeth!" He whispered in that lewd manner, snapping his jaws together playfully, and dropped her hand, closing the sliding door. "You need me, call," he added and climbed into the driver's seat.

The sky had darkened quickly, enough for his headlights, and Aino finally exhaled as the van left the way it came.

Wilholm was too handsome. Too charming. She could easily fall in love with him. It would be a wholesome, desperate consumption, and that would be the end of that. Aino would be stuck in the North just like her mother twenty-five years ago. Frozen in place until she melted and regained her senses. Aino left the bags on the porch and returned inside, only the trees watching her smirk at the thought of Wilholm and his courtship.

Mattias was already distributing steaming hot chocolate to the newcomers. The Japanese couple sat by the fire's hearth while the Americans and Australian woman stood, examining the Lappish-folklore paraphernalia her father hastily nailed on the walls. They were mostly relics her grandfather made or bought through the years for himself. Aino's eyes often drifted to the large painting above the fireplace as if it was magnetic. An unknown, behemoth beast silhouetted by the frozen landscape of forest and river. Though big and bear-ish, its edges were nebulous and it wore odd, strange antlers. Aino knew her grandfather, not six months dead, would absolutely be pounding the wood of his casket if he knew his paintings and carvings were now used to entertain filthy foreigners.

The back door opened and the last guest entered. Tall and slender, dressed as a typical German hiker, he was really the first arrival hours earlier in his own SUV with Carly. A lanky and blond German with sharp features and a sharper chin. Not *un*-handsome but… different. Kurt Muller wiped his hands with a begrimed rag, a sour look on his plain features as he studied his dirty palms. He looked up though and the expression was replaced with a congenial smile, like a mask slid over the disgust, and he gestured outside.

"I cut down that reindeer and put him in the shed."

It struck her as odd that he would be so nonchalant about hauling a butchered body and she was about to say thank you, but Mattias interrupted, handing her an empty tray.

"Mister Muller! Please join us, let me introduce you and your girlfriend to the other guests," and he shepherded Kurt to the others.

Aino followed. When Muller abruptly paused in stride, she nearly ran into him with her tray. She looked up. The American bear-man and Muller were staring at each other, the latter's blue eyes wide. Before she could ask if they knew each other, the moment had passed, and Muller moved to the fire with Carly, his long arm wrapping around her. The six foreigners, grouped in a picturesque tableau, presented the strangest assortment of characters Aino had ever witnessed in the frozen North.

"Guests, this is Rocky and Regina Armstrong," he gestured to the Americans, standing apart and dwarfing the others with their size and ostentatiousness. "You already know your friends Mister Tetsuya Hiraki-san and his wife, Mimiko." The Japanese couple, sitting somberly and awfully posture-correct, bowed their heads slightly with no smiles. "But this is the other potential investor, Kurt Muller, and his girlfriend, Carly. They drove here for a European road trip!" Her father laughed good-naturedly and Aino glanced between the American and German man to see if they claimed familiarity, but each studied his cup closely.

Regina Armstrong ignored Mattias's introductions and interjected, "Mattias, sweetheart, my phone isn't working. I was getting a signal at that little landing strip and a way through the drive, but nothing now. I know you wrote little-to-no service, but I thought you were jokin'!" she exclaimed, holding a chunky phone glittering with pink rhinestones. Mattias held up a finger like a teacher making excuses to parents.

"Yes, I am afraid the reception is not wonderful, especially in storms and strong aurora. But! But! I have spoken with Telia Carrier and they have agreed to install a new tower, especially for our future resort!" He said this enthusiastically, pausing cautiously before continuing, "And we also have plans for–"

The Japanese man finally spoke, his English immaculate with an aristocratic twist as he skillfully interrupted, "Mattias, it was a long flight, would you please show us to the rooms before we have any presentation?"

Her father blinked for a moment, perhaps stunned by the weight and hefty tone of Hiraki-san, as if each of his words was carefully chosen and carved with precision. But a smile came quickly to Mattias' round, happy face and he opened his hands, palms spread wide.

"Of course, of course, friends. But I am afraid you do not have 'rooms'." He paused for dramatic effect, a circus performer reeling in his audience. Indeed, the six guests frowned. "You have glass igloos!"

A murmur of excitement rippled through them, finally giving her father his desired response, and he beamed proudly while gesturing they should follow him outside. "They are a five-minute walk down a sledding path and we have push-sleds for your bags."

The others rose, depositing mugs on Aino's tray without thanking her, and dutifully followed. She also exited just as Mattias slid the last of three sleds forward, and the couples stood waiting in the porch's front light. Aino flipped a switch inside the door and all around the driveway, a line of electric torches shone brightly, casting the looming trees with stark, bizarre shadows.

The American and Japanese women began taking selfies together in front of the snow-clumped trees. Mimiko's poses were demure in contrast to the boisterous American, arching their backs, holding peace signs with their fingers on top of their cheeks, and Aino pondered how such a friendship began.

Mattias loaded bags onto the sleds without the men's assistance and Aino stepped down to help.

"Can you start dinner while I take them?" he asked, his voice low and perhaps worried.

"Yes, I can cook, you know," she replied, hinting at what was once a sarcastic teenager.

"Well, I don't know what you learned down there. What your mother let you forget, I don't know anything," he muttered, uncharacteristically bitter, lifting the last bag onto the sled and turning to their guests with a new smile.

"Gentleman, if you could help and push one of the sleds, I'll guide you to the *new* igloos!" he exclaimed, the showman returning, and began leading them to a narrow trail, steeped in pitch and out of the torchlight.

Aino watched them leave, some trudging laboriously through the pack, the Japanese and American husbands pushing their sleds while her father controlled Muller's. Regina and Mimiko had intertwined their arms and followed last, giggling over something private when the American stopped in front of Aino. She removed her glove and plucked something from her outer pocket, holding it to Aino.

"For the bags." Regina smiled and Aino squinted at the American money between her french-tipped nails. Aino's gaze, however, lingered over the large and dark bruise peeking beneath the wrist line of Regina's coat. Distracted by the mark, Aino blinked herself to focus.

"No, Mrs. Armstrong, that's not necessary." The woman shrugged and replaced the money, continuing her pretzel arm-in-arm walk with her friend. Aino stared at them, still dazed by her father's retort.

Eventually, the strange assortment of guests were consumed by the darkness of the trail, enfolded by the pines, and the wind rose to make her shiver. It bit her cheek enough she felt the burn in it, and Aino had a moment of fervent wishing that this failed. That her father would appear too sycophantic, too desperate, that these investors would not be interested and there was no money elsewhere. That his dream and prospects would fail. Die before they ever breathed. Oh, that would be ideal. Then she could leave with a clean conscience and return to civilization and a warmer south. A wind racing to the Barents Sea skirted through the trees, bathed in great white hoards of snow, branches bent like old men with humped backs. Watching her and judging her like cranky old men, just like her grandfather who always spoke such strange things as if they were riddles. The huskies' howls floated to her on the porch, their cries nearly human amongst the frozen trees. She fucking hated this place sometimes.

REGINA

A slender crescent moon radiated an odd wintry bucolic-ness over the forest. It was only 3 pm and it sat low and tenderly in the sky, bouncing off glittering snow as it crunched beneath their boots and caked the trees like buttermilk frosting. The scenery was picturesque, a dang Hallmark movie, and Regina always flicked the TV off when those came on. Mimiko tightened her intertwined arm, pressing their bodies closer as they walked in the frosty air. The pines were densely packed on either side of the trail connected to the driveway. Too far from the others for eavesdroppers, they still spoke in Japanese.

"That was the owner's daughter?" Mimiko asked, glancing over her shoulder as they entered the treeline.

Regina nodded. "She didn't live here when Daddy and I visited." A shiver ran down her entire body, her three layers feeling like one in this goddamn frozen shithole. Regina's body was so harmonized with Texan heat, reveling in the beneficial properties of sweating out your body weight in water, she didn't even use AC in the Dallas mansion. She continued thinking over Aino, maybe five years younger than herself, ruminating on the young girl's presence.

"She's from Helsinki, I think. She does not look like a 'wild' woman, does she? Too frail."

"What about the other one, the girlfriend?"

Mattias's headlamps created bulky shadows of the four men and one woman far ahead, and Regina assessed 'Carly'. An unknown, her name too simple for someone who seemed complex. She recalled watching her forearm flex in the lodge and thinking there were too many muscles there.

"I don't know. She is new. She seems... sturdy."

Amused, Mimiko murmured. "You still notice the strangest things. 'Sturdy', 'frail'. No wonder I never beat you in chess." She exhaled hot breath. "I have missed you, Re-chan." She rubbed her friend's forearm as if trying to transfer heat between all the high-tech wear and Regina grinned in the hidden darkness, leaning her head on Mimiko's shoulder. Her free hand began reaching for Mimiko's stomach but thought better of it. They couldn't speak of such things in the private jet.

"How do you feel?" she quietly asked.

Mimiko's arm stiffened for a fraction of a second until she casually replied. "I got rid of it."

Saliva pooled in Regina's cheeks and bile rose in her throat. Regina's poker face was perfect, good for investors, gambling, and suppressing trauma, but this shocked even her, her lips falling open like a river trout. She was the only one though. In the dim light, Regina recognized Mimiko's standard expression of Japanese indifference. A mask. She hadn't even paused in stride, speaking of her abortion. Voices ahead on the trail rose and a putrid, unbearable thought entered Regina's mind. So heinous, so infuriating, her voice quivered.

"Was it... him?"

"No," Mimiko replied quickly and confidently. "He doesn't know."

The others had stopped, listening as Mattias spoke gaily of local legend. The women joined them and Regina's thoughts were quickly displaced by the nearest tree. Bloody streaks were carved and scratched into its frozen bark. Mattias's headlamp shone brightly on it, the dark red crimson of frozen blood contrasted against the brown trunk. The others glanced at their arrival, Tetsuya's head turning only slightly, and her spine tingled knowing he subtly watched them.

"Is someone... hurt?" Mimiko asked.

Mattias laughed. "Oh no, no, it's the reindeer! I guess I could say some legend or fantastic tale. Maybe Otso! The Bear King of the forest scratching his claws!" He laughed again and Regina winced at the irritating sound. "But no, the reindeer are shedding their antlers for the year and they rub them off against the trees. Like an itch. I don't know whose this is though!" He stared at it for a moment longer with a curious expression but then showily laughed and resumed walking, the others following. Regina paused by the tree and the two women examined it, her eyes wandering over the black and gray bars of trees behind, watching slender shadows phase in and out with clouds crossing the sky.

"Hard to forget this tree, huh?" she murmured and Mimiko agreed with a confident nod.

The tree's bleeding streaks turned black as Mattias's light receded and his inane chatter resumed. "...will love them. Maybe you saw two by the bridge? They have been trained for sleigh rides! Can take two people at a time and are very energetic!"

Mimiko remained silent and Regina wanted to ask why she did *it* but remembered Tetsuya and his alert ears, and the more she thought it over, Mimiko's reason was obvious.

After a minute of slow walking, the darkness of the forest lessened.

A thick ribbon of overcast clouds signaled a clearing ahead. The line of stoic trees ended for an expanse of luminous white. Sitting a hundred feet from the trailhead was a line of three glass-domed igloos, spaced thirty feet apart.

They were majestic with interiors glowing cozy yellow light, conflicting with the surrounding snow and night sky, and as kitsch as a Kincaid painting. The bottom row of glass, chest height, was hidden by dark curtains, and Regina's interest was immediately intrigued at the voyeuristic quality of the igloos. If the lights were on and the inhabitants standing, every*thing* would be on display. But they were charming and exotic in an unfamiliar, arctic manner.

Regina and Mimiko approached the others, already organizing themselves. She raised her voice to the annoying octave. "Oh Lord, this is beyond cute, Mattias, what a hoot! I ain't never seen anything like it, huh, Rocky?"

Her husband didn't answer and pushed his sled ahead, aiming for the last igloo in the row, but Mattias spun and addressed her, thrilled by her enthusiasm. A hungry dog for a bone. "Thank you! Yes, yes, as you see, there is much space. We cleared this field nearly, well, nearly ten ye–" Mattias's wide smile dropped abruptly, his words stuttering, and Regina and Mimiko gave him their whole attention. Regina's face piqued and her eyes narrowed with his slip up. He quickly recovered his thoughts, speaking louder for the others moving to their igloos, "And... there is room for another 37 igloos!"

Claiming the first and nearest igloo, Tetsuya left his sled and held his hand out to Mimiko. Regina's poker face returned when she recognized the fleshy, shiny end of his pinky finger. Gone. Chopped off.

"Mi-chan," he gently commanded, and Mimiko obediently unwound her arm from Regina's and into his, leaving her friend cold.

Mattias continued his salesman spiel though no one had stopped to listen any further and Regina slowly trekked in her husband's tracks. "You'll find the bathrooms stocked, but there are only some twenty minutes of hot water at a time."

The husbands and Muller ignored Mattias now, their willingness to be polite and remain outside in the dark arctic air completely evaporated, and he called louder, "And... and, I have not installed the locks yet, but since we are only eight..."

Tetsuya and Mimiko entered their igloo, and Regina patted Mattias on the shoulder in a friendly, pitying fashion. The fool smiled briefly, more concerned with the men now gone. "Yes! Please return to the lodge in...an hour? An hour, yes? For a short walking tour."

The girlfriend, Carly, lugged her small weekender bag into the doorway as Regina passed the middle igloo and they shared a brief nod before the other's eyes moved up and down her, stopping at the fur-lined and very expensive boots. The corner of Carly's mouth tipped up ever so slightly, mockingly, in the foyer light. Instead of shooting steely arrows with a vicious glance, Regina continued, plodding easily through the deep, soft snow, sinking half a foot with every step. By the time she arrived at the last igloo, Rocky had hauled in the last of her many bags, his head ducking low through the long and narrow arched entryway. A glacial wind rose, tossing her hair and burning the tip of her petite nose, and she followed.

The dome was spacious and warm after being outside, with a carpeted floor and a queen bed sitting up the back. Open doors for a shower and bathroom sat opposite the front entryway, built into the circular design, and a wide shelf lined the entire circumference.

"Fucking hell, you can see *everything*," Rocky mumbled and Regina turned to the glass. Kurt and Carly's igloo beside them, perhaps thirty feet away, was a beacon, clashing against the inky woodlands surrounding the open field. The pair moved inside the igloo, perfectly clear behind the thick glass and oblivious of their audience. They talked casually, clearly at ease with one another, and Regina briefly wondered how the pair had met. The igloos were serried in an angular line, Mimiko's and Tetsuya's mostly hidden from view.

"Well, yeah, I guess that's the whole point? Just imagine when the sky is lit up..."

Rocky, however, was already on a rant, his hick accent turning deeper when he was mad. "That asshole lied about the landing strip.

Two fucking hours in a van? No one's gonna wanna fly *and* drive that far for a resort. Even if they do have a private jet."

Her back turned to him, Regina rolled her eyes, then squinted at the surrounding plain, cupping her face over the glass. With the light inside, the forest simply stood as a mass of pitch. An endless void stretching forever and to nowhere. "Don't be so sure, babe. It is *very* appealing to get away from the masses these days. If it was a full service you could just relax, scream existential dread right into the trees." She zipped open her suitcase on the bed. It was *very* appealing.

He ignored her, "It won't make any money, the return isn't enough..."

Regina sighed and unpacked her boots. The Yaktrax, with their steel spikes for climbing, had caught on her white turtleneck. "Babe, you have to think long-term with these investments. It literally takes *years* for a full return of capital. But if you're a founding investor, the dividend yield is gonna be just crazy, hun."

Rocky grunted and Regina glanced aside. Shit, he was thinking, his face a cro-mag puzzle. Jesus-fucking-Christ, was it the word *dividend* or *yield* confusing him this time? Since recently investigating the last decade of expenditures it was clear he was still learning the oil business. Hell, his credit card showed 'Business for Dummies' purchased only five years ago. She untangled the crampons from her sweater, wondering if they even had the capital anymore, when Rocky stumbled over her ski bag on the way to the bathroom.

"Oh geez!" she exclaimed, "Sorry, hun, let me get those tucked away, yeah?" Regina went to her knees quickly, heaving the heavy bag aside for him.

"Why the hell you even bring those? Not like there're any mountains or runs around here," he scoffed, "goddamn waste of space bringing shit like that. And white snowsuits? How the hell is anyone gonna find you if you get lost? You go for a walk, stumble, fall and break your ankle and it'll take us hours to actually see you. Sometimes you got no horse sense, Reg."

Regina exhaled frustration and pushed to stand, mumbling, "Says the man who brought no long johns to the Arctic Circle."

She said it beneath her breath. A whisper. She was so sure, Regina didn't even notice his silence. She did, however, notice his lower, deeper voice when he next spoke.

"What did you say?"

Regina winced when the lights flicked off, and she spun. His black silhouette rounded the bed in a slow, measured stride, stiff and towering. A strange mix of electricity and unease and excitement and anxiety ran through her cold body.

"You think you're smarter than me?"

"Rocky, I was just jok–"

"Take off that suit."

"Babe, we're in a *glass* house." Regina glanced at Muller's lit igloo, the pair still unpacking and talking amicably, nicely, as a couple new to each other did. Not when a couple *really* knew each other. Not when couples grew on each other like festering black mold.

"Please don't..."

He hovered closer. "Take it off or I'll fuckin' *rip* it off. And that's the *second* time I've asked."

Regina's mouth clamped closed. She could fight back. Allow years of frustration and shame to explode like a bull from the rodeo gate. Maybe give as good as she got with her new French tips. A scar. But everything had a time and a place and it wasn't in a glasshouse. She sniffed away tears and diligently unzipped the front of her suit, shucking it from her shoulders and exposed a sweater over a thermal top and long johns on her legs. About to sit on the bed to untie her boots, Rocky was abruptly behind her. His wide, calloused palm grabbed a fist full of her hair and extensions and jerked.

She hissed through her teeth and his strong forearm encircled her waist like a python, lifting her effortlessly. He walked to the side of the dome, the shelf in front of them. Rocky was strong, and what was once a turn-on was now a curse. A man who could lift a woman could also throw her around.

He dropped her, the snowsuit bunched around her ankles, her legs trapped. His strong arm pushed the back of her head forward, her whole body bending to lean over the shelf and into the curtain. The glass was only an inch away as her forearms held her from being squashed against it. Regina's whole body tensed, muscles unconsciously fighting though she shouldn't, it would make him angrier. And enthused.

Her warm underwear was yanked without hesitation, revealing warmer and smooth skin, until it sat on her thighs. The slick, watery sound of spit smacked into a hand. He slapped her in the way he always did and she winced, shuffling her legs further apart, still bound by the suit at her ankles.

A thrust, nearly irate, certainly excited, pushed Regina further onto the shelf, a brief pleasure running through her until her hip bone ground against the shelf's wooden edge and the top of her head hit the curved window. She braced herself with a hand. The gap in the curtain parted and revealed their crude position should anyone be searching the confines of their dark igloo. She reached to close the curtain but Rocky quickly snatched her wrist. His rough fingers, the fingers of a once-blue-collar laborer, dug into the bruise he'd bestowed last week, pressing her wrist into her own lower back and holding it down.

He thrust again and the top of her skull hit the window, "Black!" she exclaimed. Another thrust, another thunk against the glass. "Jesus, Rocky. Black!"

"I heard you." He breathed calmly, her head ramming into the hard, insulated glass. Through the curtain's gap, Kurt and Carly were laughing, oblivious. The punishing rhythm was constant, and Regina squeezed her eyes shut, pain throbbing in her head and genitals, more bile rising and laced with thick hatred. Rocky would kill her one day. Maybe it had been his plan all along. Likely not with any of their guns or hunting weapons, but she bet it would be with his own hand. He grunted, exertion toiling his athletic body.

No. Maybe he wouldn't.

Not if she could do it first.

Kurt Muller and his girlfriend hugged, and Regina saw the faint lines of the first igloo through them. The chopped-off pinky finger of Tetsuya flashed in her mind. It could be worse, she thought, tuning out Rocky's sounds, the scent of his musk, his sweaty skin slapping, and thinking of other things. Happier things, happier people, sakura floating from the sky. It could always be worse. You could be married to a foolish Yakuza with no escape.

Well, there was always one escape.

TETSUYA

The darkness of this wilderness was unnatural and alien. Slender silhouettes moved within its gray ink the longer he stared. Only shadows, small, infinitesimal motions, but Tetsuya was astute at feeling eyes, and more than once the hair on his neck had stood erect. He examined the tall vertical lines of the close forest one last time from the doorway. Gentle light beamed everywhere and from nowhere, the fresh snow gleaming radiant despite only a sliver of moon behind low clouds. But the forest...

The Southside with the trail was shielded from the wind and therefore the trees were barren of snow. Tall and layered in black and gray, shadows within shadows shifted in the breeze, and Tetsuya recalled Aokigahara. The suicide forest. Spirits lingered in forests. They were harbors for malcontent afterlives. A forest stowing spirits was as natural as the sun stowing heat in the beach's sand. His hair stood again and he knew eyes searched for him.

He shut the door, the latch silent, and turned to find Mimiko, watching him. She lowered her eyes and began undressing her outer layer. Slow and somehow cautiously. She still removed clothing as a Geisha, though she had only been one for a year before retiring to marry. A rare breed. Shy, coquettish. Rituals and ingrained sensibilities from years training as a Maiko, an apprentice, still controlled her every unconscious move. Tetsuya's face contorted into something akin to displeasure.

Mimiko was respectable in every way until she reunited with her high school friend. Howling like baboons and stumbling into one another like gravity set them adrift. In the five years since they married, the women had only seen each other three times, and each time Regina plagued Japan and stayed in a nearby hotel, he instantly regretted allowing it.

Mimiko turned, laid her phone on the shelf, and removed her white snow pants, unexpectedly mesmerizing her husband. All of a sudden he wanted the bare skin of her neck. Clean, smooth, regal.

His hand reached for her shoulder, stopping an inch away when the cut nub of his last finger neared her porcelain flesh. The new ending still gleamed raw pink, tight and stretched, even three months after being cut and cauterized as his first warning. His hand quickly retreated, reaching for the suitcase instead. Heavy and rigid with its metallic frame, he dropped it onto the bed.

"You are too inappropriate with Regina. Too many champagnes on the flight. No more," he said plainly. Mimiko simply turned her head, her profile displayed with her petite face unreadable, but she nodded once. He unpacked a set of warmer clothes from their suitcase and began removing the ones he wore until abruptly remembering the glass igloo around him, his head swiveling left.

The igloo beside them, the German and his girlfriend, was illuminated. Even though the downlights were low, Tetsuya still witnessed everything above their waists. Their lips moved, their faces happy and enviously carefree as they unpacked. But with the distance, the thick glass, and the wind outside, it would be doubtful anything could be heard even if they screamed.

"Do not undress except in the bathroom, yes?" he clarified, her back still to him as she faced the black Northern forest.

Mimiko turned, her expression incredulous as it flickered between the German's igloo and his stare. "Of course."

She muttered as if he were a simpleton for even mentioning it, and his jaw clenched ever so slightly. A cruel memory of her first reaction witnessing his new wound burned behind his eyes. Scorn turned to an ugly defiance and mocking. Her adopted arrogance and elitism rearing, Mimiko became unwaveringly insolent whenever the American visited. Less reserved. Less like a wife. It was distasteful. They held stares and he unzipped his outer shirt, slowly pulling it away. Mimi's eyes frowned at the corners but didn't turn as he undressed, pulling the tight fleece over his head, exposing his naked and lithe body. Her eyes lingered on his tattoo sleeves.

The devil-red Oni, fanged and snarling, wound with flames around his right bicep and stared at her when he flexed. His left arm rippled with the Phoenix, new and still tender with its vivid fan of feathers. She nervously glanced at the neighboring igloo, then to his dark gaze trying to burn the insubordination out of her. Tetsuya's chest remained unadorned, showing the smooth, taut muscles of an enforcer. He would likely not be allowed chest ink until higher in his organization. He stepped forward, two meaningful, slow steps. Intimidatingly, agonizingly slow and purposeful. Their eyes never left each other. Mimi's body remained relaxed, but he noticed her breathing paused with those two steps. He gently pinched her soft chin.

"You become too much like a schoolgirl."

She swallowed and exhaled, contrition on her features. "I am happy to see her, that is all. It has been two years since she visited."

He searched her hazel eyes and she promptly bowed her head to the floor between their bodies, his half-clothed.

"You should have remained in Tokyo. Perhaps you will stay in the igloo tonight. You are jetlagged."

More insolence brimmed in her eyes, the purse of her lips, and he released her chin, turning away before he became angry and did something permanent. Tetsuya was no good with emotions, sad or angry and the few between. He always did something regrettable. Permanent. He looked to his decapitated finger.

"But we need this. We need to start making money after..."

His head whipped around and his stare cut her enough to snap her beautiful mouth shut. "You do not worry about money, Mi-chan. Yes?"

She nodded once and he exhaled loudly, displeasure in the very breath. His fingers itched to do something. He readied for a shower instead.

"It's just that... we were invited because she is my friend. Mattias invited us because Rocky suggested us. It will be strange if I am absent on the first night..."

He undid his snow pants, allowing them to drop, and Mimi's pleading ceased. "I will think on it," he replied, then entered the small shower beside the outer door. There was no bath in the small space. But the water was hot, scalding, and though the shower stall was cramped with the outer wall of the igloo curving into its frosted glass, it would hold two people.

Tetsuya washed his body, his hair, scrubbed his feet, ridding himself of every iota of recycled air from that private jet. Hot water seared away the memory of the frost and after scrubbing, he simply stood beneath the rain-like showerhead.

A strange noise, a *swoosh*, sounded outside the igloo's glass, loud enough that Tetsuya heard it above the water. His head turned to the frosted wall and he briefly thought of his katana, hidden within the metal struts of his suitcase. The only reason he'd agreed to a private flight with the tedious and brash Americans was that private planes rarely had suitcases screened.

He opened the shower door with the water still running to find the igloo dark. A light nimbus of clouds hung over the clear glass. "Mimi? Did you go outside?" He asked. Naked, he stepped into the small foyer, dripping, and his feet trod onto trekked-in snow.

Tetsuya's heart pumped slightly faster, thinking his wife was gone, when she suddenly appeared, also naked. The shower's light shone on her. Her long hair, black and shiny, was freed from its traditional tight coil and splayed over the large koi fish tattoo encircling her lower right shoulder.

"No," she replied, and her freezing fingertips pushed him into the shower, closing the door behind her. She inhaled as if breathless, like she needed air, like she was excited and nervous and the change in character warmed his heart. Her arms, freezing against his hot skin, circled his neck, and their bodies pressed together until her back was flush against the frosted wall and water snailed between them. The wind howled outside on the cold vista, carrying the wail of the dogs on it.

KURT

"So, you like to watch, huh?" Carly said in a lewd, salacious tone, and Kurt looked away from the Hiraki's igloo, now dark for some time. She ducked her head from the tiny bathroom and shook her hair out. Wild, frizzy curls brushed her shoulders. Her voice returned to its normal, jovial one with her thick Australian accent. "I always heard Germans were kinky, but never thought I would be lucky enough to strike it rich."

"Oh no?" He grinned and snatched her arm, yanking her into his body and toppling them onto the bed, a flurry of her untamed hair and his long limbs. The bed abruptly creaked and shifted, something breaking in the frame, and the pair stilled with shocked faces until all at once they began laughing.

"Oh God, that father and daughter are gonna think we're freaky sex addicts."

Kurt smiled at her again and tenderly lifted himself off her body and the bed. "I'm German, remember? We are all kinky sex addicts. They knew what to expect."

He kneeled and inspected below the bed, pushing aside his large weekender bag, and immediately saw one of the bed's slats had simply shifted off. Pushing the mattress up, he replaced it with a grunt, then noticed the bottom compartment of his bag slightly open. The zipper had pulled open somehow and the nozzle of his gun's silencer glinted chrome in the dark gap. He zipped it up.

"Fuuuuuck, Holymotherfuckershit, it's cold!" Carly groaned comically and the bed above shifted. Her feet, covered in cute little socks with kangaroos on them, dropped to the floor on the other side while she fetched another jumper. Kurt stood and watched her search for another layer. The way she bounced from foot to foot like a ridiculous bunny, it was impossible to not feel something more than lust for Carly, though he tried his hardest. She exclaimed, "How do people live like this?" and pulled out another thin shirt.

"Wait, don't put on any more of that cotton. You need wool for the top." He crossed the room, plucking out his own clothing. "Heavy and warm." The sweater was miles too big for Carly, an athletic woman's medium to his skinny and tall, but he pulled it over her head anyway. "Can't have you freezing to death up here, can we? Terrible fifth date protocol." Her head popped from the neckline with a new, serious expression–something akin to shy, though he was still learning all her tells. "You know, this is the craziest thing I've ever done."

He paused for an infinitesimal, flustered moment, unsure of what 'craziness' she referred to, before unfurling the jumper down over her layers. "What? A road trip to the Arctic?"

"No–well, yes, never that, but the whole, just take off and go on an amazing, once-in-a-lifetime trip with a man I've only known for a month and met in a Berlin cafe kind of thing." She wrapped her arms around his waist and stared up at him with a dreamy smile he hadn't seen before. An endearing smile touching every inch of her face. He frowned internally though a generic grin remained stuck on his own.

Carly was becoming attached. And he didn't seem to mind. It had been the plan all along, a new girlfriend, the blissful 'honeymoon' stage of a relationship. Get her good and devoted and ready to defend him should anyone inquire. But now he also felt something stirring that shouldn't exist.

His digital watch opportunely beeped, saving him from an answer. Kurt looked to it, then rubbed her arms up and down. "Right, an hour's nearly up, we should get you fully dressed." He pulled away from her grasp and she loudly sighed before flopping on the bed and rolling over.

"You know, it's becoming painfully obvious you're a control freak."

He pulled out a pair of warm hiking boots, more flexible and better for activities like running and climbing. He frowned at her and she laughed.

"Okay, maybe not a control freak, maybe like, just normal OCD. Or really really organized." She glanced to his side of the shelves with his clothes in their neat rows and he sat facing them, about to pull on his boots, also arranged straight. She suddenly lunged, clamped onto his back like a spider, and whispered in his ear, her hot breath tickling his lobe: "Makes me wanna just mess you up a little."

Shivers ran from his ear all the way to his groin, a long, devilish cascade of desire rose with her challenge. Carly liked rough. No, not rough, forceful. She had shown herself surprisingly strong, and she liked someone equal. He reached behind his body and swiveled in a fast motion, pushing them back so he was on top of her again. She immediately struggled with good humor, trying to break his hold and leverage him off, their groins grinding invitingly as they wrestled. In the month of knowing each other and since sex on the first date, attraction wasn't an issue, and he uncharacteristically unzipped the fly of his snow pants and began pulling hers down.

"I can get messy sometimes."

Her eyes opened, surprised, but then she began to frantically wriggle her pants off. "Now, with the lights on?"

"They'll never know, and I'm German, remember? Kinky."

Fifteen minutes later, Carly and Kurt rushed to catch up to the others, already out of their igloos and trudging down the path. At first Kurt was irritated with himself, impulsively wasting time. He always preferred to be first, see what he was walking into, and satellite imagery could only show so much.

The temperature had dropped further. The air was the kind of crisp that stole Kurt's breath, as if he had jumped into ice water. But with their long legs and light feet, Kurt and Carly soon saw the backs of Regina Armstrong and Mimiko Hiraki in the faint light of their head lamps. They walked intimately with intertwined arms and slower than the husbands who had decided not to wait for them. Carly was surprisingly fast and light in the packed snow, and he had the notion she might be faster than him. They stopped some ten meters from the pair of women, unnoticed as they were deep in conversation, easily heard in the quiet snowy forest.

"*Muzukashi, hai,*" Regina said, shaking her head. She had changed into a different sleek, all-white suit that melded her body, almost camouflaging with the snow. Her friend replied, the pair continuing their conversation in Japanese, and Carly nudged his shoulder, making a face to show incredulity. It was then that Regina noticed them walking behind, turning and nodding in their direction before facing forward once more. They fell into silence as the head of the trail and the wide driveway neared.

Mattias stood outside, in the process of lighting several old-fashioned kerosene lamps, handing one for all. He fumbled lighting the last of them, and the blundering motion gave Kurt the distinct impression he rarely used the antique lamps. He reached it out to Kurt with a shaky, feeble hand.

"Wonderful, wonderful! Now we are all here, we can go for a very short walk before a wonderful dinner, yes?" He nodded, and Kurt noted the desperate look in his eyes and felt a strange pity for the wannabe hotel connoisseur who would likely never get his money or amount to much more than what he currently was. How sad to always want to be something out of reach, to want to be something other than you were and perpetually unhappy.

"Work up an appetite, yes!" Mattias continued. He held an open arm out to the side of the lodge, a well-worn path delving into a wall of snow two feet high. The couples began walking. Tetsuya Hiraki took possession of his wife's arm and placed them first to follow Mattias. The three couples paired up. Tetsuya kept a close grip on his wife, the two stepping in time with eerie precision like soldiers off to war. It was doubtful the Japanese gangster would leave his wife often or for long periods of time in the next week.

Kurt made to step in behind the Asian couple, closer to Tetsuya, but abruptly stopped for Regina, who nearly accidentally backed into him. Rocky's face amusingly flashed with worry, as if he only just remembered it wasn't smart to show his back to Kurt. But Regina had already begun walking, and he followed dutifully.

They walked through the backyard, passing the shed where Carly had somehow convinced him to get his hands dirty and help out, stowing the reindeer carcass, and continued on the path weaving through the trees like a fat, long white worm. Arm in arm, the three couples walked two by two, Mattias playing an incarnation of a bumbling ferryman, a guide in the strange dark with his lantern raised. Once or twice he would stop at a fork, looking left and then right for too long before taking confident steps up one of the paths, mumbling apologies such as 'Aino usually feeds them' or 'everything looks different in the night, yes?'

At first they walked in silence. The smothering muteness of the forest and the cushion of snow was disarming after the cloistered quality of the igloos. But the group must have become inoculated and little whispers began.

"Is it like you remember sugar?" Rocky asked his wife, his conversation, or rather his voice, loud enough for all to hear.

Carly pointedly interrupted them. "You've been here before?" she asked, tugging on Kurt's arm so they neared the Americans.

Regina turned her profile slightly, her full lips pursed. In the lantern's light, she exhaled a ghost of irritation, quickly replaced with her smile. "Oh, yes. My daddy and I took a European vacation some time ago. He and Mattias even met and we got the grand ole tour. I was very young though, I can't remember much of it. But he loved it here, so different to Texas."

Mattias had briefly stopped the whole procession to listen to Regina's answer, the only sound among the trees, but quickly returned to walking with a quicker pace when she finished. Kurt's brow furrowed under his beanie, and a brief wave of guilt burned him as he thought of the geriatric oil tycoon, laying on his own couch and clutching his chest. But why was she lying? Regina wasn't *that* young when she and her father made their trip over. She had been over fourteen, and they had stayed a few days.

As if Mattias suddenly realized he was responsible for their entertainment, he began some kind of rehearsed monologue, perhaps recounting facts rather than storytelling. The group trudged along, Kurt noting the sound of his boots on the old, crunchy snow. Not too loud if he tread in the other's steps. Beside him, Carly kept curiously quiet, not out of breath in the slightest. He watched her out of the side of his eye. She licked her lips, and the warm glow of the lantern gave a pleasing softness to her face.

He mentally shook himself. *Pay attention.* Mattias had begun speaking animatedly ahead. "... of course, The Finns love nature and it's made many crazy...though of course fantastic, stories of Gods and whatnot. Tapio and Mielikki, the God and Goddess of the forest, always fighting with others over the Sampo..." he drifted in and out, Kurt's ears drawn to other sounds in the forest.

The seven sets of footsteps, the smacks of random snow clumps falling from trees, the *scuttle* of claws from little creatures crawling up permafrost trees. While most trees were thick pines and conifers coated in layers of frozen snow, some were barren and bare for the winter. Branches like lithe and bony fingers reached for the group on the path. The innumerable and ubiquitous trees, the winding path, all looked the same to Kurt's city eyes. There were no indistinguishable or remarkable features like a city. A bagel store, a smoke shop on the corner, the waiting black sedan. This was going to be harder than he planned. A job out in the middle of the wilderness sounded like an easy and anonymous wire transfer, but then he realized separating from the crowd would always be difficult when there was no crowd.

"Holy shit," Carly whispered, and Kurt's glazed eyes focused as he brought himself out of planning. Ahead, Mattias had stopped monologuing and rested his lamp on a tall wooden post, the start of a fence holding a small clearing beyond. There was the *huff* of heavy breaths from many great beasts. Several pairs of glinting gold eyes reflected the lanterns in the strange arctic darkness. Kurt placed his lantern on top of another tall fence post, a makeshift lighthouse, and the glowing eyes approached. Several reindeer emerged from the gloam, smaller than horses but bigger than a mule. Three had antlers with long, fleshy strips of velvet hanging like rags, the bloody bone beneath exposed. Kurt could only blink at them for a moment while Carly gasped.

There were five in total, maybe another two shadows hanging in the recesses, and they approached Mattias, holding out his hand as if offering food. Carly reached her arm through the wooden bar fence to try and touch the nose of an approaching female.

"Crap, these guys are cute! I mean, kinda, right? But they look so small, can they really pull a sleigh?"

"Oh yes! One for every person with a good sleigh. Maybe two people, but not for long rides." Mattias cheerfully gestured to the shed, the outlines of sleighs in its eaves.

Kurt began trailing around the fence, interested in how many reindeer actually lived in the pen and if they would be of any use. Releasing them as a distraction? Abruptly, the distinct feeling of an observer grazed his neck and he turned ever so slightly. Tetsuya Hiraki was examining his back, subtly but surely, and Kurt fumbled with reading glasses from his chest pocket, putting on a show of squinting while cleaning their lenses. He stuck them on his face and peered over the fence.

A beast walked to him, red-velvet rags swinging, thinking Kurt would offer it food. The pen was large, and the lift-up gate for entry was over the other side near a small lean-to shelter. Kurt began returning to the others, when a marking on a tree, a little higher than his own height drew his interest. He raised the lantern.

A crude blade, possibly a Sami knife with its wide edge, had once carved a rudimentary drawing into the old tree. A reindeer stood proud, a giant halo circling above its antlers, its carved eyes were deep like they had been stabbed rather than cut. Kurt fingered the carving, its edges worn and eroded, the image itself was buried in the tree as if the bark had grown around it. The carving was made years, possibly decades, ago.

"What's this?" he called, interrupting Mattias once more, though he didn't think anyone still listened to the old man.

Mattias also raised his lantern, which formed a warm glow over his rotund face and congenial smile. It turned to an unhappy frown a moment later as he studied the carving and the jowls of his cheeks sagged. The others also took interest, circling the tree.

"What's that circle above the antlers?" Carly asked, her gloved hand reaching and gently touching the reindeer's hoof.

Mattias cleared his throat, "I think... that would be a luonto, a part of the soul..." He laughed, too trill and embarrassed. "Finnish lore is so silly, you know. Always with the nature and the land." His demeanor then changed from embarrassed, and he raised his hand like a school teacher explaining to the class: "A person, a family, has guardians that are part of their soul, a luonto, and that guardian is connected to the land. I think. There are so many contradictions, you know!"

"Shit! Aren't we having reindeer for dinner?!" Rocky Armstrong laughed at the back of the small crowd, guffawing.

Instead of being further embarrassed, Mattias' face lit up. "Yes! You are right, we only eat the small ones, the young ones, for food, though. But now you say it, Aino must surely have dinner ready, so let's cut our tour short. That pathway to the East leads to the husky's pen, and we will visit them tomorrow. But I am sure you are all hungry, yes!?"

"Well hell, yeah!" Rocky said enthusiastically, the tall man stretching himself out and showing his impressive girth.

Kurt looked up the east pathway Mattias briefly pointed to, trying to imagine it in his mind. His photos had been taken in the summer, when the trees were thick with feather branches and shielded the pathways on the ground. But he knew the only other structure was some small shack five hundred meters away.

Mattias began leaving. Mimiko and Regina lingered by the pen for a moment, the two openly talking in Japanese, the words too fast and harried for Kurt's limited vocabulary. They then hooked arms and followed Mattias and Rocky, now asking questions.

Tetsuya shot the women a furious look, a murderous glare, before he also silently followed. Carly spun, forming a large 'O' with her mouth and her eyes widened at Kurt, pointing out Tetsuya's reaction. He stifled a laugh at her expression and obvious bravery. Fuck, he was glad that bastard's sword had stayed in Japan. Heat and displeasure radiated off of him like nuclear waste. He would resemble a cornered animal now out of his element. They all were. It was why Kurt accepted this job.

Carly studied the tree and the carving once more as they were about to leave, the reindeer in the pen already wandering away, turning into silhouettes among the darkness. When she was finished she pulled him forward to follow.

"Can you believe that American bimbo can speak Japanese? That shit is hard. She must be secretly smart or something," Carly whispered, her voice bordering a chuckle.

"Oh, I don't think anyone here is just what they seem," he replied, also in a whisper, wrapping an arm around her shoulder as he led her on. He should know.

He wasn't German at all.

MATTIAS

A small trickle of translucent blood seeped from his steak. Mattias subtly pried open the flesh of his dinner, noting Aino hadn't cooked the meat properly. Too rare. An embarrassing and lewd pink. He nervously glanced at the others' plates, most already half gone. The Americans were nearly finished. Just as well; the cold made people hungry without them even realizing it. The cold silently sapped one's strength like a hidden leech.

The small tour of the lodge and its dark surrounds had gone well. The guests even showed interest in the reindeer carcass laying in the shed on their return and asked Aino about the process once inside. But so far dinner was not the amazing, gourmet meal he envisioned for a high-class resort. Certainly none of the showmanship or food designated 'cuisine'. Aino certainly did not take after her mother in the kitchen.

"So, Mattias, those dogs barking..." the Australian asked and Mattias' worry left. He blinked at the young woman, maybe a little older than Aino. She reminded him of what Aino would be like if she stayed North. Strong and resilient. Not so disgruntled and with a smile always nearby. Not so 'city-ish'.

Carly deepened her brow at his silence, sitting across from him. For some reason, the two heads of the table had been occupied by the American and Japanese man, sitting long ways. Mattias hadn't protested like his father would have. Guests came first.

"The dogs barking..." she pressed.

"Yes, the huskies, of course! Tomorrow we can meet them, very lively animals!" He rose quickly, wiping his mouth with his napkin, and opened a clunky and large pine cabinet close to the grand dining table. Inside was an old TV system in dire need of upgrading. He pressed the worn buttons on the remote control, and the CCTV connection flickered through the staticky screen. The first camera, secured to the far interior edge of the kennels, displayed a panorama showing ten separate wire cages where his huskies were housed. Their floodlight, in a tree high above, flickered with an occasional shadow, signaling wind strong enough to wave entire branches.

"I only have five, but as you see more cages are ready. Very sturdy cages, otherwise they would run wild!" Mattias's stubby finger pointed at the black and white dog, easily camouflaged on screen. "Five is good for one sled. Much faster than the reindeer. Two, maybe three people." Mr. Armstrong frowned at the number, his wide mouth turning completely downward. "But it is a good start," Mattias pressed on. "Then, when we have more guests, more dogs, more sled rides, more money."

Damn. He mentioned money. He wasn't supposed to, not yet. Don't let them think of money, reel them in with the resort, the forest, the vision. Don't let on how much he needed them and that damn foreign money. Luckily, the Australian interjected and pointed to the screen.

"Where are they, exactly? They sound so close, and why do they... howl like that? They sound...human." She grimaced.

Mattias laughed. "Yes, they do. We say they are 'singing'. Huskies are very fun. Very social dogs. If you kept walking up that path and left, their cages are another two minutes. Tomorrow we can walk there and let them run. Maybe try a sled."

The women's faces lit up, the men's became thoughtful. Mattias's stubby fingers fumbled for the next channel and the reindeer camera flickered onto the screen, a night vision camera, surprisingly affordable. The enclosure the group had visited earlier flickered to life; the large wood fence pen, encircled by trees, was far below. The several reindeer of the Järvinen family huddled together in the far corner as temperatures dropped. They were not nearly as interesting as the dogs and he flipped the channel back.

Mrs. Armstrong rose from her seat and approached the TV. "My lord!" She smiled broadly, American orthodontics gleaming with wide eyes lined by clumpy mascara. Her finger touched the huskies jumping around on screen, smudging their cages. "How many are there, did you say? How fast can they go? Rocky and I like fast, though I'm guessing they probably can't pull... Oh gosh, I just had a thought, y'all have sleigh's with sleigh bells? Like Santa's sleigh over mountains of snow? Dee-lightful!" She laughed.

Mattias laughed also and clapped his hands together. This was the response he hoped for, excitement. He was at first anxious when Rocky Armstrong, and Regina by association, showed interest in investing, reaching out to him shortly after his advertisement. But maybe in the decade between her visits, her memory of the trip with her father was nothing but happy. He patted her shoulder and held an arm out to the other end of the room.

"Yes, yes, Regina, dear. There are seven dogs and five reindeer in *that* pen. And of course we have mountains and lakes! The most beautiful lake! Frozen now, of course." He and Regina crossed to a large table beside the Christmas tree he had put much effort into, and then he dramatically pulled the sheet away to expose the miniature of their land and the future resort. Making such a thing cost more than anticipated; little houses and little igloos cost an arm and a leg. He would need to sacrifice thousands of arms and legs for the real thing. Chairs scraped over wood and the others followed.

"Is this...?" Regina questioned.

He answered promptly. "Yes, this is Järvinen land, the same you visited all those years ago." He pointed to the borders of the table, "All two hundred hectares of my family's land wedged between national reserves. Pristine!"

The other guests surrounded the wide table and he breathed deep, recalling his practiced spiel and trying for genuine rather than desperate.

"As you see, there is the field for the igloos, an easy five-minute walk through the woods." His finger directed their eyes to their miniature blue lake with the future canoe hut and water sports. "In summer, a kilometer, a ten-minute walk through the forest, is the most sacred lake in Lapland. Bursting with antiquity and ancient legends! A land of Gods and sprites!" He added grandeur to his voice, his arm waving up and towards the fireplace where his father's own painting hung.It was a majestic panorama of mountains and lake, a figure of a large deer in the forefront.

Mr. Armstrong smirked with his wide mouth. "Any of that true?"

Mattias grinned back. "Of course, there are legends of this land. There are legends everywhere for everything. Everything from little gnomes, Menninkäinen, to willow-wisp. My father knew them better, the best, but then again, he was of an older generation. Another kind." He briefly peeked at the oil painting of Ukko, grand Father-God of the sky hanging near the door. The Father-God stared at him disapprovingly.

"Mattias, how come your land is undeveloped? It is beautiful, and with a water feature," Mister Hiraki-san asked as if there was a catch, a secret to uncover. Mattias's mouth parted like a caught fish.

Regina spoke instead, her voice full of mischief and a hint of curt sourness. "Mattias, I distinctly remember being yelled at and chased by some crazy hermit when we visited. I think Big Daddy was even sore at him, ruining some kinda deal or prospects? He was straight up a bear after that, miserable to live with."

The others looked at him, many eyebrows arched, many smiles turned to frowns. Mattias laughed, though sweat trickled down the back of his shirt. He tried to sound amused and light.

"Oh my, yes, that must have been scary for a young girl. I am afraid that crazy hermit was my father. Vinha Järvinen. And to answer your question, Mister Hiraki-san, it is untouched because he wanted it that way. My father and I did not... see eye to eye. Is that how you say? To be truthful, he even stipulated the land to be forever undeveloped in his will. But I was able to overturn it shortly after." Mattias' throat tightened and he made sure to not glance at Aino, whom he felt watching from the kitchen. It was undeniable that Aino had her grandfather's eyes and could uncannily replicate his withering stare when desired. "He was quite mentally unwell and the courts agreed."

There was silence, heavy and awkward, hanging like a paternal, weighted blanket on Mattias' shoulders. The Father-God and all his creations stared at him from the walls.

"Dessert!" Aino called cheerily and the moment passed. The guests turned to steaming bowls waiting on the table. "I'm sorry to interrupt, all my fault. But in my opinion, Mustikkapirakka is better warm." She smiled gently, and Mattias thanked those old Gods he didn't really believe in for sending him a smart daughter.

Smart daughters were nature's reparations for silly fathers.

"Ah! Yes, warm blueberry pie! She is absolutely correct. Cold is no good. Already too much cold. Please, please, friends, let's return. We'll discuss the land and resort with after-dinner drinks, yes?" Mattias shepherded the group back to the table, the ghost of his father remaining with Mattias's model table, whoring his ancestral lands and Aino's birthright. Wind rattled the windows as Aino sat at the far end, between Tetsuya and Muller. Her phone suddenly beeped in her pocket and drew the attention of the quiet table.

"You have reception?" Regina quickly asked, rabid for an answer.

Aino read her screen with a faint smile. "It comes and goes. I am on a carrier operating also in Norway." She motioned to the window. "I have found the less wind, the better reception." She held the screen up for the rest of the table. A bright rash of red with a dark purple and black center smeared across a map of northern Finland.

"But the reception was enough for a brief moment to let us know there will be beautiful Revontulet tonight. I am sure the wind will push these clouds away." Aino spoke surely and Mattias was once again thankful for the little salesperson in her, even if she denied it. At first, with those eyes, Mattias thought she also inherited her grandfather's spirit. An environmentalist, a preserver of the past, and a xenophobist because he wanted all others kept out, to keep the land and riches for himself. Then her mother asked for a divorce, and it appeared Aino simply suffered a youthful apathy to everything.

Missus Hiraki-san spoke, her voice soft and curiously sonorous, an actress projecting to a small theater. "I'm sorry, that word, 'revon..' that is not English, yes?"

"Ah, no. She means the aurora. 'Revontulet' is the Finnish word meaning 'Foxfire'. The Lappish believed a magic fox ran through the sky, his tale shooting sparks that are the aurora."

"Is that what your father believed?" Regina asked, spooning a mouthful of pudding.

Mattias's smile faltered but quickly resumed. He now regretted even mentioning his father. Even in death, his eccentricities lingered over the lodge and the land. "He believed many things, but *only* one about the aurora? Who knows? There are many strange tales. Most say it is a gateway to the other world." He made sure they knew he didn't think much of it by chuckling. "There was one I remember about women covering their hair because the lights could pull your soul up and steal you from this world."

His guests showed interest with raised eyebrows and pursed lips but there were no further questions as they ate dessert and Mattias was happy for the silence, a reprieve. After a few minutes of quiet, private conversations, a comfortable mood settled over the table.

Mister Armstrong asked quietly, "You mentioned the lake? Something about 'sacred'. I gotta tell you, Mattias, I've had to deal with some of that shit back in Texas. All those indigenous tribes. Protesting and all that over 'their sacred sites'. Makes my skin crawl thinking about all the hoops they make ya jump through just to shit on some of that land. You ain't got nothing like that up here, right?"

Mattias required a long second to process Armstrong's ridiculous accent but replied with a smile that hurt his cheeks, as if the question was most ridiculous. "No! Oh no, the Sami Homeland is further East. The land is, *was*, sacred to my family, the Järvinens. Once upon a time. My ancestors, my grandfathers, made many stories of the lake and the family being 'one' with its spirit, whatever that meant. They say our guardianship comes from its waters. 'We are it'. Most likely to solidify land claims, I guess. 'The land *owns* us' is what he used to say, and we have been here for centuries, apparently."

Mister Armstrong frowned, deep lines around his wide mouth, and Mattias laughed. "Do not worry, my friend, there are no 'native' people here to protest a wonderful resort... And the only person to resist, my father, is quite dead."

Wood scraped over wood. "Mattias?" A firm voice interrupted and the two men turned to the other end of the table. The Japanese couple had stood, unique figures with their perfect postures. "Where is the bathroom in the lodge again?" Tetsuya asked.

"Ah! I am afraid the bathroom is yet to be upgraded and it is still an 'outhouse'." He gestured to the back door. "But we extended the porch, so it is just off to the side. A nice little space inside. Quite warm and upscale"

Aino dutifully stood, her arm showing the way, and slender Mimiko followed, her husband tailing her as if he would keep guard in the frigid air. Mattias spoke to their backs,

"Mister Haraki-san." The couple turned, "There is no need to..."

A heavy hand rested on his forearm and he looked at Rocky's face, imperceptibly shaking. Mattias glanced at the Japanese couple, already on their way outside. Only when the door closed did Rocky release his hand.

"Sorry, partner, that's a real-life yakuza right there. Real protective of their wives... and property."

Mattias's nose scrunched, confused. "A what?"

Rocky leaned back in his seat, his tall, athletic frame stretching, a stark contrast to Mattias's hunched posture. "A Ya-ku-za. Like a fucking Japanese gangster. Like real you-don't-wanna-fuck-with-kinda man. Don't think I've heard of one leaving the motherland though. Think I heard Reg muttering something nasty 'bout him last year. Something like he was a fuck-up. He must need the cash-flow bad anyhow."

Rocky's voice was intrigued and mysterious only to turn serious all at once. "Meaning, you don't want to accidentally lose any of *his* money."

Mattias's entire body went rigid and his mouth dry. Rocky leaned forward with stern eyes, the warning clear. Mattias stuttered, uncomfortable memories resurfacing of the large amount of money used for clearing the field only to be disrupted by his hostile father returning from vacation. "You spoke to Regina's father..."

The seriousness left Rocky's face and he resumed his relaxed posture, "Ah, fuck. That ole oilman said lotta bad stuff about everyone before he croaked, even his own kin. Doubt half of it's true. Course I don't give a rat's ass 'bout the past. But I do need to double the last of his money, understood? A Texan with guns is just as bad as a Yakuza with a sword, and Reggie and I own a shooting range. Visit twice a week."

His deep twang dropped with the last sentence. The V in his forehead deepened, and a sinister quality overcame his features, his gaze darkening without ever moving. Mattias swallowed the lump stuck somewhere behind his tonsils and gently nodded. The tense moment passed and they looked over the rest of the room in silent agreement. Regina had left the table and wandered the space, her attention consumed by the reindeer antlers hanging above the coats and keys.

"That is a strange friendship, between you and the Japanese couple. You recommended Mister Hiraki-san, how do you know such people?"

Rocky scraped the last of his pie from the bowl, metal scraping ceramic. The man had handsome features, sharp cheekbones, a clean, shaved jaw, and big lips. He smacked them together and motioned to his wife.

"Regina and Mimiko were high school friends when her daddy sent her off for a year abroad. He was too soft on her, you know? She got into trouble doing stupid shit, pickpocketing, and whatnot. Let her do whatever the hell she wanted when she was younger on account of her momma dying from a heart attack, I think. Got into his head somehow that Jay-pan was a strict, safe place with all their study-abroad highschools and she would be outta his beard for a while. As long as she wasn't getting arrested was his way of thinking."

Mattias wanted to know more about the... yakuza. Was that like the Italian's Mafia? Criminals? He couldn't use criminal money, could he? Mattias didn't know the first thing about criminals and how they used their money. Laundered? Laundered money? Unless this money wasn't 'dirty' and...well, a lot of money. Maybe if it was a lot of money, more than his asking amount, he would accept. He needed some income soon. But he was a nervous type of person by nature, a by-product of his authoritative father, and such illegal things made him flustered. He was no good at confrontation after his few harsh lessons. He considered carefully how to broach such a tender subject when Rocky leaned in again, this time, his voice hushed.

"What about that... German? How do you know... how was he invited?"

The young couple, the German and Australian, had retired to the fireplace, and the men studied them in turn. Their carefree natures were written in their body language. Young and relaxed, they were a nice addition to the unusual group, though they made everyone seem brusque and sharp in comparison.

"Mister Muller? He also answered my postings on the investment site, shortly after you. He is an IT manager from Munich. Trying to get into investments, you know. Trying to get his start." He frowned and examined Muller closer. A lanky figure with a close-shaved head, he wore thick tortoise glasses he hadn't walked in with. His girl-friend, Carly, was of similar height but had a sturdiness in her body and face. Curly hair was pulled into a relaxed ponytail and she wore no makeup. They laughed together and it was... endearing. They looked so young.

"Actually, you know, I'm not even sure if he can afford the 'buy in' fee for the resort."

"Oh, he can afford it," Rocky murmured, and Mattias turned to him questioningly. Rocky continued staring at the couple, unwaveringly until he turned to Mattias with a wide, leonine smile that was somehow disarming. Like Mattias wouldn't dare not to smile back.

"Come on, Mattias, let's look at this model and you can tell me the ole nitty-gritty of this 'sacred land' shit."

TETSUYA

Mimiko laughed a strange, high-pitched sound, nearly a giggle. The wine glass in her hand sloshed on account of Regina touching her forearm as they shared insipid nonsense. The American's laugh was brazen and crass in his ears, a donkey's bray. Every time she swished that long, fake hair, petting and twirling it between her fingers, Tetsuya had the pleasurable daydream of taking his katana from his belt, shearing her long locks off, and throwing them in the fire right in front of her.

But his sword remained in his igloo and it was too late to regret allowing Mimi to join him tonight. He had a weakness for her subservience and she knew it enough to ask the right questions at the right time. He would rebuke her later. Maybe with the flat of his sword on her backside.

"So, let me ask, is it Mister Hiraki-san or...?" the German asked and Tetsuya returned his attention to the surprisingly boring and harmless man.

It *was* a surprise. At first, Tetsuya was wary as he entered, wiping blood off his hands. His attuned instincts rang alarms, but then waned through the night with observation and halting conversation with the unassuming figure. Muller, constantly pushing his heavy glasses back up his nose, had yet to have anything interesting to offer for discussion, and his voice was dull. Like he was trying to make Tetsuya sleepy with leaden thoughts. They were trading pleasantries simply because both desired the warmth of the fire with all the seats occupied and his girlfriend was engaged by the young Aino. Tetsuya faked a tired grin, the best he could do, and looked up above the mantel to the painting. It wasn't done particularly skillfully, but it held gravitas. The animal in the front, a deer, was large, and something was wrong with its antlers. There were too many, and they were too big.

"Simply Hiraki-san. Mattias forgets 'Mister' is what 'san' means. It is like he is saying Mister-Hiraki-Mister."

The German chuckled, searching for the man in question and finding him at the model table, answering Rocky's questions with thoughtful expressions and pointing fingers. Tetsuya frowned. He had important questions in his notebook and began patting his chest pocket when across the seating area, Regina stood, giggling and wobbling once on her feet. The woman had drunk too much, as usual. If it wasn't ume-shu it was champagne, more air for her head, and now whatever swill Mattias served.

In Armstrong's private jet, the old friends had sequestered themselves in the back, speaking with hushed voices, playing chess and helping themselves to the liquor while Rocky slept and Tetsuya discreetly watched them reunite. Regina had won three games of chess, using her Queen for every challenge on the board. Once he figured out her simple strategy, Tetsuya was tempted to play her but then remembered it required being close to her.

Regina zipped up the top of her jacket and switched on the headlamp on her head. "Okay, I'm going to try for this 'outhouse', wish me luck. Dang, I'm already cold," she said to no one in particular and anyone who would suffer her. She left through the back door and his eyes drifted over the men at the table, staring at them for a few moments. Rocky Armstrong had his hand on his chin, studying the miniature, his thoughts clearly running numbers.

Tetsuya should be doing that. Asking questions, smart, informed questions. He needed to start earning money in the next few years. Big money. He wasn't a *chinpira* anymore but Tokyo was too big, he was always left behind because he couldn't multitask. One thing at a time. He was, frustratingly, only good at one thing at a time. That had been proven and paid for.

He patted his jacket pocket again and remembered this was not the same coat he arrived in. Mimi had rightly suggested this coat was warmer than the one he wore on the plane, which held his little notebook of questions.

Tetsuya placed his whiskey glass on the mantel and nodded to the German before approaching his wife, speaking in Japanese. "I'm returning to the igloo for a few minutes. Do not move from the fire, yes?"

Her cheeks were rosy with heat and wine and the merriment in her eyes died a little when he told her to stay. Still, she kept her amicable smile and made a pronounced movement of sinking into the deep chair. "Don't be long."

He bent to kiss her head, inhaling sakura shampoo. Mimi didn't acknowledge the kiss, her dreamy stare on the fire. The ladies opposite were deep in conversation and now all three men stood at the model table, conversing about financials. He should hurry.

Donning his thick jacket, gloves, and hat from the front hanging rack, the layers so thick his movement was restricted, he exited the lodge. The wind howled with husky song, tussling his short locks, and he studied the sky. The young daughter was correct and the clouds were now dispelled. The clear night sky stared at him and Tetsuya was struck still on the porch stairs, hypnotized by innumerable stars.

Tokyo was a wasteland for the wonder of the night sky. The neon horizon of the metropolis flooded the atmosphere with a miso soup haze. Its pollution spread far to the outer cities, even as far as Fuji-san. Even in the mountains, the city's pollution reached.

But this...it was nothing like this. He exhaled a cloud of hot air laced with awe. The sky was a painting, a hyper-realistic version of reality. More real than anything he ever witnessed. It was clear and fresh and alive, the stars twinkling in harmony in a great cosmic chorus. Tetsuya's heart flipped, the effect immediate.

Yes, absolutely yes.

Tetsuya would transfer Mimi's remaining Geisha money and whatever he could borrow and hustle and scrape and buy a little piece of this. This was living. Alive. He felt alive all of a sudden, his heart progressing to somersaults.

He stepped down the first stair and a rustle across the driveway snickered through the trees, breaking his bewitchment. In the drive-way's fluorescent lamps, the faded-orange of a foxtail disappeared beneath a bush, and black beads glinted at him through brush. For the first time on this trip, a grin curled his mouth, as he watched the fox, the kitsune, an animal common to Japan, scurry in the snow.

The wind ran through the clearing with steel-cold fangs, reminding him why he was outside at all. The faint howls of the dogs continued riding the wind and Tetsuya listened. They did sound like humans in their more fervent cries. Humans wailing in pain, only to sing it out. He trotted away from the lodge and down the forest path, the gloom of the path and forest a great contrast. Only a few meters in did he realize he forgot one of the many headlamps hanging on the other side of the door. Tetsuya hesitated and waited, his eyes adjusting to the unique dark. Just like the open clearing, the trail through the forest glowed with an unusual luminosity. The trampled snow reflected the vague night above, radiating starlight and besieging the dark undergrowth.

It was not a long walk, less than five minutes with long strides, maybe two if he could bear the searing cold in his nose and run. He quickened his step through the terrain of snow, his lungs working harder for the pace and effort. His breath billowed and the air was curiously still within the trees, sheltered from the wind. He was so loud in his own ears. The path bent right and he looked to the sky, hoping the gale wouldn't regress and lead more clouds to block the stars, when he halted a second time.

A light swelled in the sky riddled with stars, weak and as slow as a calm heartbeat at first. A pulse of faint green followed by another beat, though maybe it was really Tetsuya's own heart. The faint green light slowly emerged as if a veil of a color, newly created and never seen, was being draped over the trees, brighter, more ethereal with each thrum of his pulse.

The aurora.

Foxfire.

A ribbon of strong emerald light waved above the trees, running vertically and along with the path, and Tetsuya exhaled. It was clear and vivid as if paint had smeared across his eyes, scoring into his memories and past lives. Unearthly and spectral, it struck him where he stood, watching something bigger than him, grander than anyone, occur above. The clear sky was one thing, this was another. If the clear night sky and a million stars could make a man believe in life, the aurora could make a man believe in Gods.

Tetsuya swiveled on his boot heel, his first instinct to rush and tell his wife, to share this ephemeral phenomenon. He was certain it would bring them closer, sharing something otherworldly. Tetsuya had a sense, an uneasiness, it could disappear at any moment; a gift easily bestowed was easily taken. Much like Mimiko. He made to return when a flickering gleaming caught his eye.

Deep among the trees off trail, a fluorescent light flashed. His exhilaration a moment ago abruptly dissipated with the flickering light in a strange and odd place. He studied it, partially obscured by rows of slender and thick vertical trunks like bars of a prison. It was one of the headlamps, judging by its size and color. It swung side to side in the inky dimness.

"Hello?" he called to the light and it swung wider in response.

He stepped forward and off the trail, his boot crunching snow and sinking half a foot deep. Tetsuya eyed the light, judging it only ten meters away, three trees in. He squinted, hoping to pierce the darkness made from the towering canopy. Though strong above, the aurora's glow accomplished little beneath these trees. His nape tickled in the familiar sensation and the light swung faster as if an invisible hand hit it. He called again.

"Who is there?" His voice echoed and Tetsuya realized the silence in the forest was now absolute. The errant sounds of a snow-covered wilderness were gone. The creak of branches laden with ice, occasional plops of snow falling to the ground, a rustle of a night creature. All disappeared.

Dead air.

Cold, dead air.

There was no one here. No one living. No one could be living in a forest as quiet as this. Tetsuya remembered Aokigahara. That forest was also silent—a silence he once revered when he buried a victim or arranged them as suicides. Silence meant solitude. He was all done with those types of jobs since the last one went poorly and the man he had been tasked to kill had escaped, and Tetsuya's worth diminished greatly, paid for with his finger tip.

Wind breathed through the treetops, only a sliver of hush high above him. No. No one lingered here except for ghosts. Perhaps a sleeping spirit, waiting for its own time. Tetsuya stepped further off the trail, confidently stomping through the snow, mud to his boots, and to the light. His bold, heavy tread was the only noise in the forest.

He reached the lamp. Its elastic band hung from a broken branch just above his head and he examined it. It swung only slightly now, its momentum draining. It was a very new headlamp, the same as the lodge's, and instinctively, he searched the surrounding area for moving shadows. Camouflaged figures waiting. His breath held, the air before his face crisp and clear.

There was no one. Not even those ghosts. He looked directly up, the aurora blazed overhead, silhouetting the black spindly crown of branches in spectacular green light. His mouth literally parted at the splendor, remembering he had to tell his Mimi. A black shadow moved against the green, certainly not a branch. Slender and fast. A glint.

Metal sang against hushed snow and teeth ripped away from the tree.

In an instant, crisp, smooth steel ran into his open mouth, dissecting his tongue, punching through the back of his throat and down. Burying like a knife digging into a flank.

The darkness, a figure of ink, dropped lithely from the branch, a great weight released that shifted falling snow, and something deep within Tetsuya's chest ached with a soreness he had never known. Tender and stiff. His knees buckled and the steel remained lodged, stuck, in his mouth, choking on the sharp coldness. His teeth scraped the metal, opening up his throat, down through his neck, and below in his chest, holding him rigid. Skewered. The blade juddered again, angrily.

With watering eyes, he could only stare up at the immaculate light of a green heaven. His gaze grew dim at the edges, and his brain recognized the handle of the sword lodged in his mouth, his breath fogging the cold metal, and wondered why it was no longer in his suitcase.

MIMIKO

"The edge is the border of your land?" Mimiko softly inquired. Her gaze roamed the corners of the model with its little green trees, her fingers gently circling the delicate brim of her wine glass.

Mattias nodded. The Finnish liquor, a rough minty flavor, had gone to his cheeks, ruddy and full like apples. For the first time, Mimiko felt like if there was one person she would use the word 'jolly' for, it was this Finnish man desperate for their money.

"Yes, yes, Missus Hiraki-san. The land is a rectangular plot, one of the biggest privately owned in our region, a narrow strip between government-owned parks."

She scrutinized the model. Mattias wasted 80% of the table with trees. Their igloos and the lodge were close to a corner of the table, meaning they neared two other borders and the start of Järvinen land. Her eyes followed the little driveway they traveled earlier. In reality, the main tar road lay a ten-minute drive away, passing woods and a small bridge covering an icy, black river.

The model was designed for summer and more agreeable seasons. On the table, the river, painted aqua-blue, serpentined through the tiny plastic trees and along a quarter length of the table until it met a small lake, in the lower quadrant of their land and at least two hands' span away from the lodge.

Aino joined them, handing her father another small glass of clear liquor he accepted with a happy-drunk smile, his cheeks bunched up. His arm encircled her shoulders and squeezed affectionately, the first demonstration of such between the pair. Mimiko's gaze slowly wandered to the fireplace, flames licking high. Regina stood beside it, warming herself with hands raised. Her sculpted, lissom body still held itself like that of an old athlete, her muscles taut, on parade. The German and Australian sitting together in the loveseat giggled at something, the levity of alcohol and affection in their tones. Mimiko returned her attention to the model, extending her pointed finger at the nearest edge.

"Who owns the neighboring land? Would he object to tourism or even a landing strip?"

Mattias's bulging red lips pursed, his frown comical on his puffy face. "The neighbor?"

Aino shoulder's straightened. "Ah, yes, you know, there was an old man in Wilholm's van today. Twenty minutes up the road? He looked... well, he reminded me of grandfather."

Mattias sighed and it was not the first time Mimiko noticed the issue of his dead father was an unwanted topic. She couldn't decipher whether it was regret or mourning, though there was rarely much difference between the two most times.

"Dressed in furs?"

Aino nodded.

"Yes, I suppose he would remind you of your grandfather. They were friends. The same type of men, really. Believed this land sacred and nothing should change on it. Stuck in the past."

His stumpy finger pointed to the border closest to the lodge, maybe a handspan or a twenty minute walk in the real world. "Sauvo Virtanen lives on the National Park. They couldn't kick him off due to ancestral rights, he is part Sami. I believe his home is close to our border, but he roams in the summer, I think. Moving with the rein-deer. 'Live-off-the-land' type of man."

The back door opened abruptly, oafish Rocky returning from using the facilities. "Y'all! Ya gotta come outside! Those lights in the sky are on! Shoot! I've never seen anything like it!" Without waiting, he strode across the large room toward the front door, pulling his thick coat on quickly.

The others followed, a bustle of many bodies by the front door, excited hands reaching for hats, gloves, and coats, then retrieving wine glasses to accompany them outside. Aino flicked a switch and the driveway's lights shut off, the darkness of the night absolute for all but the unearthly green waves floating below the ocean of stars.

Mimiko's breath sucked in unconsciously. Her heart swelled and eyes teared. A sensation of marvel overwhelmed her senses as slips of emerald silk floated over the lodge. So close and so far, Mimiko thought she could reach and caress it with her fingers. What would she feel? Cold air? Warmth? Fire? Electricity? Something deeper? Something moving around her?

A hand threaded through the crook of her elbow and Regina pressed into her. She had her tell-tale smile from when she was pleased with herself. "Can you believe this? I've never... this is the kicker of this place. The selling point. People pay a lot to see this."

"The kicker," Mimiko muttered, her eyes not daring to leave the sky should it abruptly finish. "Mattias? How long will this last?" she called.

The wind had lessened, crisp air promising its return. His arm held his daughter as they stood in the circle driveway, and he also did not look away from the aurora, but still answered. "You can never tell. I will say though, this is quite early for revontulet! If it is this early in the evening, it promises to be very strong or last some time! I do not think this is the last of it."

A strong hand possessively slid around Regina's waist, currently pressed against Mimiko's. The hand nearly squeezed between them and Rocky's thick cologne invaded her nose. "Isn't this purty, gals? Hell, this right here wants me to throw all our money at Mattias."

Regina's grip on Mimiko's arm lessened slightly with her husband's presence.

"Where's that fella of yours got'n off to? Thought he was cooking up some questions 'bout the resort in that fancy notebook of his on the plane? Sure as hell wouldn't want him to miss out on this though."

Mimiko blinked at Rocky and Regina; both the husband and wife's sharp jawlines tilted skyward. Their faces, bathed in the eerie green of nature's show, transformed their usual beauty into sickly and strange hypnotized creatures. She blinked again, emerging from her hypnosis. How long had Tetsuya been absent? More than the ten minutes it should have taken to get there and back again. Maybe thirty minutes? She unwound her arm from Regina's tight hold and placed her glass on the porch railing.

"Yes, you are right. I will check on him. He will surely want to see this and ask his questions." She passed the others, heading for the trail.

Aino stopped her. "Wait, Missus Hiraki, please take my headlamp." She turned and Aino pulled an elastic band with the small lamp from her pocket. She clicked it on and Mimiko accepted it but didn't attempt pulling it over her head with its furred beanie, instead simply holding it.

Leaving the driveway, the forest was not so bleak under the light of the aurora. The trees remained a shade of dark, but between them, the ground snow reflected light and everything... gleamed. The crunch of her boots on snow made the forest seem more than simply quiet and usually, perhaps in one of Japan's woodlands, this would frighten Mimiko. But here? Silence was natural. Organic. There was a beauty in silence, she thought. Knowing you were the only person for miles was a sensation transcending any other banal human experiences. Unlike anything available in Tokyo or Kyoto or even when she was allowed to go somewhere, anywhere by herself. Which was never.

Here, she could scream and no one would rescue her. No one would come. No one would know.

How completely alien and delightful.

The forest passed quickly, Mimiko duly noting the familiar and bloody reindeer tree as the light of the snowy field radiated ahead. Their igloo was black inside; the unusual octogonal outline of the dome was highlighted by the green sky in the background and another surge of reverence for this distant place and unworldly time bloomed in her heart.

The unlocked door opened quietly. "Tetsuya?"

Silence. Mimiko stomped her feet of clinging snow and closed the door behind her, clicking on the lights. The dome was empty and an unknown tension melted from her shoulders. She looked up through the glass. Down lights from a thin beam shone in her eyes and obscured the aurora beyond the glass, also reflecting the lamps. Could she even fall asleep with something like that above? How could anyone with feeling and eyes lose consciousness in the face of heavenly glory?

Tetsuya wasn't here and she searched for signs of his recent presence. His suitcase was pushed beneath the bed and though he wasn't the wandering type, something like suspicion tickled her insides. Maybe even excitement. She was about to leave, when the front door flew open and Regina entered in a burst, her breath ragged from the freezing air. She had sprinted to catch up. She also stomped her boots. The domes were warm, heated in some covert manner Mimiko had not discerned. Regina unzipped her snow jacket.

She wore a jet black skivvy beneath, high tech for manufactured warmth, and displayed her athletic frame. Her breath heaved her entire and full bosom, her face flushed gentle pink from the frigid air.

"Isn't this crazy?" she exclaimed, reaching and flinging her hat away, the long platinum locks splaying everywhere. They both gazed up through the glass and her hands slid familiarly around Mimiko's waist. Slender hands holding memories. She examined Regina holding her, an excited air about her. Wide eyes, blushed cheeks, a mischievous grin, and Mimiko swore Regina's heart beat frantically inside her chest. Her pulse thrummed like a frantic hummingbird.

"You're drunk," Mimiko said, grinning, her own hands covering Regina's freezing ones. The blonde's hands reached and clutched Mimiko's shoulders, one hand gripping so tight, her nails felt like the incision point for a foreboding cut.

"No! I'm excited! Exciting things! I've got a good feeling." She gestured up with her head and Mimiko followed. The corona wavered and held her transfixed as if it was a magnet and she had no choice. Her soft fingers threaded through Regina's free hair, abruptly clutching it tightly and snapping the taller woman's head downward.

"We have to talk, we need to…" Regina began just as Mimiko's mouth pressed fast and excited over hers, a tongue invading her lips, her breath gone. She tasted like copper.

She mumbled against her mouth, "Do you remember..?"

"Sakura falling like snow?" Regina replied amusedly before clutching Mimiko into her.

ROCKY

"Babe, I'm gonna get my camera, yeah? This is too perfect, B-R-B," Regina exclaimed in that annoying sing-song thing she did, pulling from his strong grip and running down the steps. Before he could protest, she had already neared the trailhead in a jog, her legs lengthening into measured and powerful strides. He watched her pert ass, round like a soccer ball even beneath those snow pants, and bit back his desire to tell her to stay. The others ignored her passing, all except for 'Kurt Muller'. The assassin's head turned ever so slightly and watched Regina leave.

What in the fuck-all was he doing here? Of all the places in the world, it couldn't be a coincidence. There were no coincidences with something like this. In the seven years since Rocky hired the man, he had aged little, though they had met only once and in the shadows of a dive bar. The expected wear and tear of a high-stress position such as a freelance hitman hadn't even given damn crow's feet to the sonuvabitch.

The back of Kurt's head resumed leaning against his 'girlfriend's', if that's what she really was, and Rocky's gaze drifted around the open space of the driveway. A tall shed of sorts sat away and to the right of the lodge. An ugly run-down wooden garage, he guessed, probably where they stored the cars and other miscellaneous shit needed day-to-day.

At the bottom of the stairs, Mattias's whole body sighed; he exhaled a warm cloud as he squeezed his daughter. He was content, likely ecstatic with his 'presentation'. Rocky stared around the space.

Goddammit, a day of travel only to discover a bad investment. Worse than a whorehouse over a field of gopher holes. It wasn't even a fraction prepared. Shit, most of the area wasn't even logged. The spaces needed clearing and it was too isolated, meaning *another* investment of a landing strip or small airport just to ensure people *could* come here. Hell, *if* all the permits were in order and tribal people or whatever they had up here didn't put up a fight for 'ancestral' shit. No, too much for too big of a risk. He needed diligence with Regina's inheritance and the rest of the company. There wasn't much left after six years of bad investments and drying oil fields, and at this point it felt like water in his cupped hands, trickling away.

The aurora yo-yoed in brightness, dimming in slow waves as it subtly snaked west and away. The four others on the ground began murmuring and Rocky sensed the light show over for the time being, or they had endured as much frigid air as possible for the moment.

"You know what, y'all? I'm gonna call it a night. Texas time is starting to hound me," he pronounced to the others as they mounted the porch.

Mattias smiled and clamped a hand on Rocky's taller shoulder like they were friends. "Okay, have a good sleep. You will wake in the dark, but we usually have breakfast at nine. Tomorrow we sled!" he proclaimed like a clown, glancing to his daughter for support. She grinned and clutched him as if he would soon fall.

Rocky smiled widely though it didn't reach his cheeks and replied with cocked finger guns. "Sounds good, partner. See you in the morning."

He met Muller's gaze and then turned away with long strides for the trail. They had skillfully avoided each other all night, though perhaps it would soon appear odd to the others that perfect strangers behaved so distantly.

Rocky's boots crunched snow like he stepped on dry chicken bones, an unfamiliar but not unpleasant sensation. The trail was still. Muffled silence clawed along his spine, and his imagination toyed with the idea of someone watching him from the tips of the trees, a gaggle of eyes high above looking down. His steps quickened. He wasn't a fast runner like Regina, but with his long legs, he could easily outpace anyone when he really tried, though he'd much rather use a swing of his fist. The end of the path neared within two minutes, a lit igloo immediately before him.

The aurora waned, now only a whisper of color in the air, a ghost of the vividness ten minutes prior, and Rocky left the treeline, his boots digging into the snow with an abrupt stop.

Not forty feet away in the first igloo were the intertwined bodies of *his* wife and Mimiko. They writhed against each other like frantic worms, their mouths fucking like pornstars. Rocky was stunned. His lips parted as he watched Regina and her best friend. Regina's hand raised to the wall beside them and the downlights switched off, their outlines melding as phantoms in the dark interior, and he could no longer place them inside. If they were still vertical.

A branch cracked in the distant forest, snow falling to the ground with a *plod,* and Rocky's unease at the forest and its isolation was engulfed in flames, disintegrated and melted with a burst of wrath and ire and the start of a confusing erection. He stepped forward, then back. A two-step. Fuck. *Fuck.* In the arctic temperatures, his blood boiled. Regina. Slut. He had fucked her till they had both come and she gratefully wept not five hours earlier. Yet here she was, desperately grinding against another pussy.

FUCK.

Another dance forward and back, his mind envisioning racing in there, pulling the women apart and making them wish they had never met a decade ago. Belting Regina with the long horn buckle sitting above his groin. Smacking that high-society hooker back into

Asia, feeling that delicate skin beneath his palm and bruising it. He paused ten feet from the igloo's door.

Shit. Where was the husband? Rocky hadn't spotted him inside, and he wasn't the type to allow his *property* to whore around.

He wasn't here. And if he suddenly arrived and discovered Rocky assaulting his possessions, then who the fuck knows what the ending would look like. His warning to Mattias echoed in his ears, you did not wanna square dance with fucking yakuza far from your own gun rack. Rocky exhaled and instead swiveled left, tramping the hard snow with his heavy boots, taking all his frothing anger out on that goddamn-packed white and cold shit.

His igloo was also dark and he didn't bother with the lights. He did pace, however, thinking over every 'innocent' interaction, churning them in his mind, making it sour and vile until he was sure Regina had lied and deceived and betrayed from day one. He had stopped the Japan trips years ago. They were too expensive for her to simply relive past glory days, drinking chu-his and gussin' up like a medieval prostitute. Rocky's gut rumbled, indigestion curling his bowels mad as they always did with stress and murderous thoughts. Light from the middle igloo flicked on, bringing him out of dark reverie.

Carly walked into her igloo, unwrapping her scarf and layers of clothing like opening a burrito. Muller wasn't with her and the idea hit Rocky so hard, he literally jumped on the spot with anticipation. Revenge held a special place in Rocky's persona. He wouldn't call it his main character trait, but one thing was certain in life. You didn't cross Rocky Armstrong and you certainly didn't make a fool outta him.

He had been so enraged Rocky hadn't removed any of his outdoor clothing, and left the igloo, his steps lighter and cautious as he passed the other igloos. His molars ground together as he crossed the first. Salacious, filthy images of his wife naked with another woman and laughing at him blazed his mind like wildfire.

The trail remained silent, though his excited breath and harried heartbeat now filled his ears and muted anything beyond. He turned the bend and the light of a headlamp illuminated the assassin's sinewy figure. Muller spun fast, whiplike, the lamp blinding Rocky, and his hand instinctively raised, shielding his eyes.

"I want to hire you again." He didn't bother with pleasantries. There were none on the first job, why should there be for a second? Even under tense circumstances and strange locations.

Muller lowered the lamp. His face showed no surprise, a dead mask almost until his brow deepened. He stared at Rocky for a long moment, and then without answering, he turned to continue examining the ground. Rocky rattled on, aware he sounded pathetic but assured by years of experience that money could cure that malady.

"Same payment, same amount. More now that the dollar's value is higher than Euros." His voice edged higher. Desperation stank to high hell on him and he could almost smell the rotting eggs of self-loathing.

Muller didn't answer, his head tilting to the side as he searched the forest floor. Finally he murmured aloud. "Who?"

Rocky swallowed, the air all at once too cold for his nostrils, burning as he sucked it in. "My wife."

Muller suddenly stopped his examination of the ground and shone the light on Rocky's face, forcing him to squint. A few seconds later, he lowered it and when Rocky's eyes had cleared, Muller had resumed his search.

"So you had me off the dad, now you want me to kill the daughter? That's pretty fucked, mate," he muttered in the light British accent Rocky had heard the first time they worked together. Rocky's eyes turned away, frustrated nothing was happening as he imagined, no immediate retribution, and was distracted by the bloody reindeer tree. Deep scratches burying blood and skin into the tree's bark. The flickering light created a moving quality in the mixture of gore and wood, and suddenly the tree was bleeding. Muller surprised Rocky by stepping off the path, trailing something with slow, methodical steps. Rocky followed.

"Look, I know it's short noti–"

"I can't," Muller muttered, distracted, not even paying attention anymore.

Rocky couldn't keep the surprise from his tone. "What? Why? It's a shit-ton of money."

Muller's voice murmured distantly, as if he was only half-participating in a negotiation. "Well, one, first the dad, then the daughter? Even if my work was flawless, a textbook heart attack, you'll have detectives so far up your ass, they'll taste your toothpaste and then mine. And second..."

He crouched, brushing soft flurry snow before picking up a short stick. In the light, it was old, worn, and moldy. Rocky leaned forward. Not a stick, thicker and decorated, made by the hand of a man. A totem of an ugly animal, squat and fat. A bear with horns. Left in the woods a millennia ago. Abandoned to rot. Muller visibly shivered, a cascade running along his body and he dropped it like it stung him. He watched it for a moment longer and then continued his thought.

"Second... I'm already on a job."

Rocky stiffened, only now acutely aware he stood alone in the middle of the arctic wilderness with a man who made a living from death. "Already on a job?"

"Mmmm, hired a few weeks ago. Anonymous. I do everything online now. Cleaner. I like clean."

"Who...who are you here for?"

Kurt Muller, surely an alias, raised his light and circled a tree, following deep footprints in virgin snow, and the men saw the third person, sitting propped up against the tree. Tetsuya's head tilted back, looking at the sky; his eyes were wide and frozen milky, and a thread of glossy blood ran from the corner of his empty, open mouth down his chin, frozen like a treacle.

"For that bastard right there."

CARLY

The women sobbed, messily, awkwardly. There was too much emotion for such a small space. Emotions amplified when they were contained in a room, engorged and louder. Maybe if they were outside...but inside, it was just too much for Carly. Even Aino, who had never met the Japanese man before today, sobbed with a useless phone to her ear. Her father hugged her, shielding her eyes from the body as he also slowly morphed into an alarming mess. Carly turned away from the small group, uncomfortable for her lack of ... empathy... sympathy? One of those emotions normal people felt when confronted with death.

It wasn't that she didn't have those emotions, grief, pain, but over death? Death was death, it happened everywhere, all the time. And death of a stranger? She glanced at the dead man, bridling her desire to poke his cheek and see if it was squishy or solid. After over an hour outside, Tetsuya Hiraki's body was frozen stiff. Bent ninety degrees at the waist, he sat up dead, all by himself in the middle of the warm room. It was flat-out weird and macabrely amusing. Mimiko knelt beside him. Her tears and body silent, her eyes roamed the surreal corpse who watched the ceiling with blanched eyes, frozen orbs, the ocular gel now solid. Mimiko mumbled a slurry of wet words, her once-perfect aristocratic English now eradicated for something rougher and more human.

"I don't understand, he...looks fine, besides that blood...how...?"

Kurt, her tranquil and quirky unassuming boyfriend of five weeks, strangely adopted an authority that made Carly's groin tingle, standing over the body he and the Armstrong man dragged inside fifteen minutes prior. A breathless Aino had knocked on her igloo door, pleading for her return, and she had stepped outside to find the other women already on the trail and returning to the lodge.

Kurt's voice was tender, his mouth parted as if the words were painful. His forefinger pointed down into Tetsuya's open mouth. "Looks like something... Struck him through. As in, a stiff line ran down inside his body."

On her knees, Mimiko's face turned puzzled while tears fell over her pale cheeks. "What? Something... pierced... him from inside?" Kurt nodded as if embarrassed. Mimiko spun to the rest of the crowd. Regina, beside the fire, had a wine glass in her hand, her face exhausted, her crying expunged, spent. She faced away from everyone and Carly had a wicked, unkind thought that it was likely because she didn't want everyone to witness her smudge mascara. Rocky was further along the mantel, the space between husband and wife far and uncomforting.

"Who..what would do that? Mattias?" Mimiko asked.

They all turned to the owner, chewing on a fingernail with wide, glazed eyes that contracted at his name. Put on the spot, he stuttered. "Whaat...I..I don't know what would do that? I don't know these things. But there is no one else on this land, no one for literally miles. Many, many miles! No one but trees and animals!"

The phone still pressed against her ear, Aino looked at him, and she tapped a button on the screen. "I still can't get through. Mattias, what...what about that neighbor?"

Mattias huffed, more worked up every second. "An old, crazy man, but harmless. Would never, even if he *could*, against a younger, stronger man…"

An awful tension kept the guests immobile, like they were also frozen in time, only their eyes flicking to one another. The red and green fairy lights of the small Christmas tree blinked methodically, and the crackle of wet wood in the fireplace overpowered gusts of wind outside. Carly waited for someone to say it. Confess the obvious thought, however suicidal it was to say it first.

There was a murderer in this room.

A trill of excitement ran down her body, electrifying her fingertips. What an unexpected day, she thought. What a crazy week, even. No one said anything though, they wouldn't dare, and she swallowed hard to keep an insane, nervous giggle from erupting. Aino swatted her hands suddenly, breaking the tension.

"*Vittu!* I can't get through, there is no signal with this wind and the aurora. I can literally hear the distortion in the line like a hag cackling in the distance."

Kurt stepped closer to the body and Mimiko. "I think we should move him. Anywhere, just not in here."

The wife's eyes were glassy in the firelight and she nodded only once.

Mattias spoke, "The shed out the back. It is insulated. Maybe he can… defrost."

Carly winced at the word, so uncouth but terribly correct. To her credit, Mimiko only sniffled. Carly bet her grief was a slow burn. A terrible, rising dawn, slowly coming and would burst all at once. She was in shock, death was never expected to these kinds of people and they were never prepared. No, for these kinds of people, death was the surprise party no one knew they were partaking in.

"I'll take him. I put the reindeer carcass in there earlier," Kurt answered, surprising her.

She stepped forward. "I'll help." Kurt looked at her with an arched brow. Together, they wrapped an arm under Tetsuya's and lifted. Carly thought lifting the man frozen at odd angles was rather like moving a small armchair–both convenient and somehow awkward to pivot. Aino opened the back door for them, the frost and cold immediately stealing Carly's breath. To the left was the far door for the outhouse, a simple but nice bathroom. Down the steps was the backyard of sorts, and thirty meters away, just outside the penumbral glow of the porch floodlights, stood the wooden shed.

The pair awkwardly shuffled with the frozen man like they were chauffeuring their drunk friend, Carly breathing hard for the unexpected heavy lifting. Tetsuya's weight was awkwardly distributed in his frozen form, though it would be a touch crude if they did handle him like an old Lazy-Boy.

"So, you seem...okay?" Kurt said between breaths.

They approached the shed, leaving the light, and a slice of wind cut the bare skin of her neck. She nodded at his comment and they dropped what was once a warm Tetsuya Hiraki. She smirked and Kurt opened the shed door, warm air escaping and they lifted him again. She couldn't help but grin impishly.

"Yeah, so I was hoping this information could wait until, I don't know, *not* a death, but I think you should know..." Kurt flipped on the overhead light and they maneuvered the stiff corpse towards the back, lowering the body and dropping him the last three inches. Kurt then also smiled, broad and intrigued for this new side that didn't revolve around their ravenous libidos, waiting for her to finish.

"...I kind of grew up on a survival compound."

The intrigue left and his face turned into a ridiculous expression of befuddlement she laughed at.

"I'm sorry, a what? You said you grew up in the outback?" They covered the sitting corpse with a tarp laying to the side. She grabbed his hand as they left, passing the reindeer carcass and washtub of liquid blood and organs pushed to the side and under a bench. The interior was not exactly warm, but not cold enough to freeze. Hiraki-san would *defrost* by morning. Carly brought Kurt's gloved hand to her lips as they walked, thinking of an adequate explanation.

"Yeah, like *real* outback. I don't know if they have that word in German. Like... a big stretch of the outback where people paid my parents to learn how to survive in the Australian bush. And when they weren't taking on clients, we lived...rough."

Kurt laughed, a new sound for Carly. Not his typical reserved chortle. She shut the shed door, transfixed by this new sound–rich and unguarded, like all their dates prior were just a warmup. He wiped a tear from his eye. "So you're like a... badass doomsdayer?"

They crossed the open yard, the dead man already forgotten, and Carly noted the well-trodden snow hid any singular footsteps. "Pffff, no, not at all. I mean, I can kill and dress a 'roo and know how to survive in extreme conditions, so badass, yes. Doomsdayer? Nah."

They mounted the steps slowly. The wind blew a great clump of fast-moving clouds overhead again and the snow lost its luminosity. "Point is, I'm used to death, especially in barren places."

Despite her serious tone and the outlandish sentiment, Kurt smirked again and shook his head with a roguish air. "'Used to death'. And here I thought you were a simple backpacker looking for a work visa. Probably something you should've brought up on the second date."

She reached for the door, his casual and charming manner infectious. "Mate, you aren't turning out to be the simple IT Startup guy either. Finding dead bodies and all. And we haven't been on much more than five dates before you asked me on a whirlwind road trip. Lucky for you I was the one girl crazy–"

They entered the lodge and were struck still by the difference. Morbid shock and sniffles had changed to tense and heavy silence. Against the fireplace, Rocky clenched his wife's wrist to his chest, his voice low and dangerous as a growling mongrel.

Despite their barely audible tones, the three others–Mattias, Aino, and Mimiko–watched from the dining table, their stares wide and unsure. Regina whimpered pathetically, struggling fruitlessly against Rocky's vice around her wrist. Despite her previous mannerisms of a strong, defiant woman, in that moment of time, Regina appeared as a cowed and helpless maiden. Carly couldn't hear her words, but it sounded like a denial of something, and Rocky's face...

His mouth sneered and the hand holding her wrists twisted, Regina's whole body following so it wouldn't break, and she yelped. Carly sprung into action, a fever of destruction rearing itself in her brain as she witnessed the much larger man hurt his beautiful wife.

"Hey!" she hollered, quickly closing the distance, her fists balled. Carly wasn't big by any means. She was, however, 5'9, trim, with wild curly hair wider than her body, and a ball of fire rearing in her belly.

Rocky's handsome but caustic face turned and lost its anger as Carly strode to him. She sensed Kurt on her heels and the American loosened his grip on the wrist but didn't release it. He spoke condescendingly, literally down to her.

"I'm speaking to my wife."

"Yeah, nah, mate. Looks a helluva lot like you are *assaulting* your wife right after a *murder.*"

Acutely aware of his spare fist stretching and balling, readying itself to punch her face, Carly steeled herself. No doubt he would. Behind the overwhelming smile in his boxy face, Rocky was the type to punch a woman, Carly was sure of it. But then his eyes flicked over her head and their burning anger tempered. Kurt, another man's presence, gave him second thoughts.

Kurt spoke. "Why don't you take a walk and cool down, Mr. Armstrong."

The largest man in the room dropped his wife's wrist, throwing imaginary jabs with his gaze at her as he left for the front door. His deathly stare then darted to Mimiko, who now comforted her friend at the hearth. Rocky inhaled a deep breath that could have ignited fire on his exhale. He flung the door open to the icy air and it slammed just as fast behind him.

Carly approached the pair of women, Mimiko examining Regina's wrist tenderly in the firelight. Mimiko uttered Japanese beneath her breath, a string of sounds unfamiliar and alien and foul exhuming from the delicate woman. Carly blinked at her, speechless for the cunning and malicious qualities in her tone, so at odds with the lady's persona. She joined them, examining the ugly bruise already rearing.

"I have a wrist brace in my suitcase," Regina said offhandedly, and both Carly and Mimiko looked at her expectantly. Realizing her lapse, she shrugged. "He does this a lot."

"Bastard," Carly muttered, examining the wrist and shaking her head. "No, it's too far away and we don't know who is out there. I mean, Rocky is out the front at least. Why don't you go out the back and collect snow for an ice pack? The thick snow is near the treeline, but still in the light."

Regina's eyes went wide, her expression curious until Mimiko jumped in and added quickly, "Of course, we'll go together... Rocky is outside at the front." Both were silent for a fraction, exchanging looks like they spoke a secret code. Then Mimiko addressed Aino seated at the table, rubbing Mattias' back comfortingly, their familial positions reversed. "Aino, would you make us some tea? I think keeping her wrist out in the cold will prevent swelling, yes? Followed by something warm against the skin? Ice then heat, right?"

Aino nodded, and the two friends left for the back door. The wind had picked up again and carried the dogs' strange howls. They gently ascended the steps, whispering between themselves while aiming for the treeline with soft snow. Carly left the door open, intending on a clear sightline, only for the wind to slam it shut. She stared at it for a moment, unsure, until realizing they would only be a minute. She joined Kurt at the one front window. Rocky sat outside on the top step, a cherry end of a cigarette flaring to life and dying with his breath.

Carly slid her hand into Kurt's, watching his glazed eyes slowly return into the room. Finally, he angled to her and squeezed their hands. "Total badass," he smirked, his German accent strangely less pronounced. She squeezed back.

"Hey, maybe I'll even take you out for another date after this debacle."

Kurt smirked and led them to the dining table. Mattias was leaned over, his forehead in his hand, a bottle of aspirin before him with a mug of tea. Aino's phone sat on the table, displaying an incomplete call.

"Mattias," Kurt said, and the older man's head lifted. His eyes were red-rimmed and raw, his face florid after too many emotions and liquor. If Carly was used to hardships and survival, Mattias was her polar opposite as a complete noob. Useless after becoming verklempt. He sniffled and Kurt spoke more kindly than she would have. "Clearly, the phone is not going to work. I've got my truck, how far is it to the nearest home?"

Talk of leaving, possible escape, sobered the owner up, and he sat straighter, wiping his face. "The nearest house? Maybe forty-five minutes? Many homes are summer vacation homes, so I am not sure if anyone is there. But there is a small village an hour south."

Aino returned, carrying three steaming mugs of weak tea, and she added, "The police station is ninety minutes, and they usually only keep one officer on at night. I am trying to call my friend, the man who drove you here."

Kurt frowned at the mention of police, and Carly glanced over her shoulder to the one window beside the front door. Rocky's mammoth silhouette had left the step, the space acutely empty. Her hand squeezed Kurt's shoulder and he followed her gaze. His mouth opened but instead of his guttural accent, a different high-pitched scream erupted from outside—terrible and coarse shrieking pain and hurt.

All heads whipped to the back door, the woman's scream slowly turning into a desperate wail, and Carly and Kurt rushed toward it, Aino behind them. Kurt flung the door open, the bright floodlights blazing on the snow and treeline. Two bodies lay prostrate beside one another a few feet from the trees.

Mimiko lay curled onto her side in a fetal position, screaming like an inconsolable toddler, a long gash across her calf. Sleeping on the white snow beside her lay Regina, disemboweled, her insides now outside.

KURT

Kurt didn't know where to look. Regina's eyes were closed, a selfish blessing on his part, her tawdry purple eye shadow still in place and immaculate. But blood copiously layered the dead woman's thorax, with viscous globs of gore, and pink pillows of intestine *everywhere*. It was impossible for one woman to have so much viscera.

Christ, he thought, *they were out here for only five minutes. Less.* The huskies were yowling, their cries distant as the breeze rose and fell like mourners at a funeral. Regina's white snowsuit had been defiled, transformed into a macabre acrylic-pour painting, and tender Aino vomited. The sound of a throat gagging threatened to set off his own, saliva coagulating in his mouth. Instead, Kurt studied Mimiko beside the carved-up Regina. Her howls had turned silent, her grief intense and brutally raw as she reached for her dead friend.

He knelt and forced himself to study her leg, her pant cut wide open. Red flesh sliced diagonally across her calf. Kurt specialized in killing people without trauma. Carbon monoxide poisoning, the time-bomb of an air bubble to the heart, a convenient but ill-fortuned snake bite. Kurt had discovered early that natural deaths commanded a lot fewer questions and a lot more money. As a distasteful byproduct of his preferences, he never had much to do with the grotesque side of death. Kurt was *clean*. He *liked* clean. He certainly didn't know a thing about *helping* victims.

Carly kneeled, mumbling to herself, "I don't understand... we were all inside. Who...?"

"We weren't all inside," he replied, and their eyes met knowingly before she went to Mimiko.

Her cold fingers prodded the bloody skin; steam rose from the wound, Mimiko's heat escaping to the Arctic. Carly was calm and Kurt watched her rather than the leg. "She should be all right, it's not deep at all. Maybe a muscle but no arteries. Help me lift her. Aino, you get the door. Let's get inside quick."

Mimiko had so far ignored her own wound, clawing dirty snow with her fingers, still reaching for Regina. She sobbed through great gasps, "*Re-channnnn. Re-chhhhann.* Please, please don't let her be hurt anymore, no more," and Kurt understood. All that blood, all those exposed organs. She would be frozen in another minute, but then her innards that Kurt couldn't look at again would draw anything hungry. A beacon in the cold, starving night. Kurt studied the ground, searching for the footprints of the assailant. A deep tread should have been leading away, but... there was *so* much of Regina's blood splashed. *Splashed.*

Aino and Carly helped Mimiko stand and instead of following, Kurt stared at Regina's face, her wound in his peripheral vision. The gash that disemboweled her was made fuzzy in the edges of his eyes. With so much blood and frayed layers of clothing, there was no telling where the wound started since her large and small intestines and other unknown organs were pushing from beneath her cut clothes in their bid for escape.

Her glossy lips were parted open. He stood behind her head and the light showed very little steam rising from her body, the offals already on their way to slowly freezing. Hooking beneath her arms, his eyes fixed to the top of her beanie, he dragged her body to the shed where he'd laid Tetsuya only fifteen minutes prior. A branch broke somewhere and Kurt realized his mistake.

"Hey! Wait up!" he called to the women nearly at the back door. They collectively turned, and Carly understood; everyone sticks together. Kurt might be a clean and efficient contract killer, but he didn't have his gun, and whatever was out here wasn't 'umm-ing' and 'ahh-ing' over gralloching any poor tourist.

But Regina was heavier than he imagined, and her body dragged leaden through the snow, a smear of red blood painting it like a smooth brush on a new canvas. He had an unkind thought of how she should be lighter for liters of blood loss and dense organs now either gone or eaten. But then Kurt remembered from old research that Regina was an athlete in her highschool and college days. Athletes were always heavier with their reserves of hidden muscles.

He opened the shed door and quickly backed in. Gently laying Regina's corpse on the cold floor beside the deer and its half-filled tub, he looked at her face for a long moment. He had watched her home for a week at some point long ago. Noting when she left for the shooting club, her social lunches, her Texan wives high-society functions. She was superficial and shallow and had far too many sports massages, but she didn't deserve this. Whatever *this* was.

Kurt quickly pulled a tarp over her and left, pausing in the doorway. Something was different in the shed. A tickle at the back of his memory nudged him that something had changed, but was too ambiguous to point at what. Tetsuya's corpse remained sitting upright, the tarp covering his body. Wind and howls filled his consciousness and Kurt shook his head, snapping the door shut.

He strode quickly to the porch when the back door flung open and Rocky's large figure filled the doorway. His mouth parted and Mimiko reflexively shied away with something close to a whimper.

Carly's entire body stiffened defensively. "Where the fuck were you?"

"I was... where is..."

Rocky was a stereotypical blue-collar thug who somehow

married into stupid-rich money by ass kissing and then killed his father-in-law via paid professional. He was *a lot* of things, but Kurt didn't think him capable of physically gutting his wife like venison. If he could, he wouldn't have needed Kurt for the Texas job. Men's weaknesses and fear for their freedom were the reason why Kurt had a steady income. The reason why society played nice. Fear of punishment was the whole reason why society worked.

But they weren't in society anymore.

Kurt stepped in front of the ladies, nearly manhandling and pushing Rocky inside, the man standing on tiptoes to see over him. The women closed the door, muting the howling dogs, and they led Mimiko to the table with Mattias, now openly crying.

"Where... where is...Reggie?" His voice clogged and made to side-step Kurt, who laid hands on his shoulders. His mouth opened and closed quickly due to lagging thoughts.

"She's... gone."

Rocky's eyes glazed momentarily, his face slack, then he blinked and focused on Kurt.

"What? Gone where?"

"*Gone,*" Kurt emphasized.

The glazed eyes closed, squeezed shut so they wouldn't betray him and show any emotion–whether excitement or grief. He *had* just asked for this. For Kurt to kill his wife. He had stomped through the forest to find Kurt, coming in hot and heavy. He had forgotten though that Kurt wasn't *that* kind of assassin. Heat of the moment, guns, a garrote, a knife? No fucking way. A gun for emergencies and a hasty Plan D, but nothing else. Kurt was efficient and, again, *clean.*

Mimiko sobbed, a soul-tearing sound that affected even Kurt's stoic conscience. Both men were distracted, and Rocky shuffled to the fireplace, dazed like someone had hit him on the head. Kurt watched his lethargic walk, a new weight on his great frame, his jacket and ungloved hands clean and blanched from cold. He couldn't have done anything to his wife. But *what* did? A claw? A talon? What could slash through a body like a hot knife in warm butter?

The Japanese wife hissed while Carly tended her leg, whispering soothing words as a mother to a child. Down the opposite end of the table, Aino did the same for her father. Curled over his knees, Mattias's words were indecipherable through the mumbling lips and a distant stare.

Aino spoke with a soft voice on the point of breaking. "We need the police. We *all* need to leave for the police."

Shit. Kurt's insides always unconsciously screwed up with the word, but it was now unavoidable. But fuck it, he hadn't done anything wrong *here*, and Carly was still going to serve her purpose of an unknowing alibi.

Carly cinched a cloth around Mimiko's calf. "A blade made that cut, I think." She turned back to Kurt. "Where are the car keys, babe?"

Kurt pressed his jacket pockets. His SUV sat in the barn, which doubled as a garage beside Mattias's old truck. Well-organized Kurt religiously pocketed the keys in his... His hand stilled over the right jacket pocket. It was too flat. The protective zipper was open, the pocket wide and empty. For the first time that night, even when discovering the bodies, Kurt's throat tightened like someone had two hands around it.

"Aino, where are Mattias's truck keys?" he asked, already knowing her answer. Intuition whispered to him and taunted that he was already three steps behind in an unknown game.

The young woman, the baby in the crowd, had dried tears, but exhaustion sat on her small body like a heavy shroud. She thought for a moment and then strode quickly to the coat rack, pushing snow coats aside in growing alarm. Beneath them on the wall sat a smaller rack. The kind for the smaller things. The kind of rack you would hang gloves on before your coat over it. Her hand reached but stopped. Aino stared at the empty rack for a long, telling moment, then swiveled to Kurt and shared a knowing glance.

"I'm going to check his room," she declared.

She rushed past the table and Carly finished Mimiko's leg. The Japanese woman laid her head on the table, silent sobs racking her body.

Carly, Kurt's well-planned future safeguard against police scrutiny, constantly surprising him, rose from the floor "What's going on now? Got your keys, yeah?"

Kurt grinned, swallowing the panic, and instead addressed the sobbing woman who'd lost her husband and... whatever Regina was... in the last hour. "Mimiko, what did that? What, *who* ... made that?" Kurt hadn't examined it before Carly's bandaging but it sure looked bigger than a pocket or even a chef's knife.

Footsteps at Kurt's back reminded him Rocky was still in the room, listening in to hear what had gutted his wife. Mimiko raised her head and Kurt couldn't help but compare the difference between her husband's death and Regina's. Dried blood stained her cheek like a birthmark, a vein of tears running a clear stream through it. She sniffled, her face still graceful even when she was torn. She shook her head and hair slid out from her beanie.

"It came behind me but was big. And fast. We were kneeling, I was scooping snow... and it came from... from around the house. I couldn't see since I faced the floodlights. But it had something on its head."

Her eyes roamed to Rocky, the 6'5" man towering above them all. She lowered her head, her shoulder jiggling up and down as all her energy directed into not crying aloud, an act that stirred a strange protective notion inside Kurt.

"What was on its head?" Mattias asked, inserting himself and speaking coherently for the first time.

Her eyes flickered all around the room and settled at the fireplace. "I don't know, I saw... bone maybe? Maybe a hat of... sorts," she whispered, another tear running down her cheek and onto her wet lips. Everyone stilled. There was silence.

Utter silence.

Impenetrable silence.

Kurt's mind, racing with possibilities and the image of someone running through the forest wearing a hat of bone, also noticed the silence. There was something different about it. Something unnerving.

"A crown? Maybe?" Mattias murmured.

"Shhhhh," Kurt interrupted, and everyone listened.

Except there was still nothing. Kurt went to the front door, not bothering for a jacket. A breeze soared inside and the great fire flickered as gooseflesh erected on his neck. The porch was empty, lingering snow drifting across the wood, and the driveway's torches shone bright against the black woods. He stepped outside.

Nothing except gentle wind.

Nothing.

No dogs.

The dogs no longer howled.

Kurt returned inside just as Aino joined them from a short hallway of rooms. Her hands flung up. "I can't find the truck keys."

Realization came quickly and Kurt went for the TV cupboard. The dead-gray screen slowly came to life as the CCTV picture emerged like a developing polaroid. Mattias moaned, a mournful, pitiful sound. The huskies' cages were flung open, the energetic dogs vanished from their small, safe enclosures.

Kurt's deft finger pressed the channel for the reindeer pen, also empty and dark. A shoulder brushed his and Aino muttered, "Why would someone release the dogs and reindeer?"

Kurt thought it over, strategy and logic warring in his head as he vaguely listened in on Aino questioning her father. "Mattias, how far is that old hermit, Virtanen, that borders our land? Would he do something like this?"

Everyone turned to Mattias at the table. Little thread capillaries, neon red, burned his round cheeks, giving him an appearance of a bawling and drunk Santa Claus. "What? No, no, to walk between his cabin and ours, well, it's at least an hour's trail walk, especially in the deep snow. He could never make that...especially in this cold."

Mattias's face abruptly blanked, the red veins draining of color as his mouth hung open, and his lips silently spoke to himself. "Bone and crown, boneandcrownboneandcrown," he murmured, his stare reaching across the room and far into the distance beyond the lodge beyond. A moment later, he abruptly curled over on the table, and Aino rubbed his back concernedly.

Sleighs and cars; it's what he would do, eliminate the opportunity before anyone thought of it. "The huskies and reindeers. No sleighs. No car keys," Kurt mistakenly mumbled aloud.

"Huh?" Carly asked.

"Aino...Does Mattias keep a gun?"

Aino, doe eyes on a young face, straightened. Her gaze wandered over the others and ended on Rocky. Slowly, she moved to the cupboard holding the TV. Crouching to three drawers below, she pulled the bottom and an old and small rifle came out, accompanied by the heavy *clatter* of bullets as the drawer's momentum rolled them out. She held the short but stocky barrel gently, and unsurprisingly this time, Carly stepped forward and accepted it, pocketing some shells.

"Where are your car keys?" she asked, checking the barrel and locking a singular bullet into the top slide-in chamber.

Kurt blinked at the fluidity and ease of her motion and instead of grabbing her by the neck and kissing her as his gut told him to, he reached for his coat beside the front door, pulling it on quickly. The rest watched him ready for outside and made for the door, Carly on his heels. "What are you doing?"

He glanced at the other four survivors, or hostages, or whatever they were. His job was technically done, and excluding repugnant Rocky, he had the urge to keep the group, and himself, alive. Well, most of them alive, if not only one of them. He looked to Carly, her wild eyes incredulous. "Left the car keys in the igloo."

"Fuck 'em, I can rig a car."

Of course she could. He zipped up his jacket and she blocked his way, the rifle between them. "Really, I can. Don't be a dickhead. Clearly, we all stick together. Survival 101."

He clasped her shoulders gently and pushed away, shielding their bodies as he opened the door. He whispered to her, a secret to be shared: "Look, someone doesn't want us to leave. The dogs, the reindeer, the car keys. I've got a rifle in my bag and I'm going to get it, right quick. Back in a jiff. All right?"

The V of Carly's brow deepened, a quirky little puzzle on her face accompanied by the tilt of a grin, like it was the start of a joke. "A rifle? In *your* bag?"

"I said I was kinky," he grinned. For all the deaths and danger and blood and grit staining his hands, it still felt like they were on a date. An odd, morbid, escape-room date with a timer clicking beyond his hearing. And it was nice. Nice for someone to be strong in the face of chaos, to share the weight. A partner. Kurt's chest abruptly warmed against the cold.

Carly's bottom lip dropped open, questions readying to explode.

"There's a lot we don't know about each other, huh?" he grinned into the side of his mouth, pulled on his beanie, and stepped outside.

The snow softly radiated eerie green, and they stepped over the threshold. The aurora had returned, brighter than before. Ribbons broadened to streams. Its slow, spasmodic waves were more of the mesmerizing display, and Kurt turned away. Sightseeing was over; the original job he had been hired for and months in planning had been done for him. A new job of continuing to breathe was now in progress.

He nudged Carly inside, reaching for the door handle. His breath thickly clouded the air between them like he expelled a poisonous gas. It was nine PM last time he checked and Kurt imagined the temperature wouldn't drop any more than its current -15 Celsius. Carly's face with her broad, wild features was close, and he kissed her with a polite amount of tongue and a mash of lips. She breathed hot air into his open mouth, smelling like the peppermint of candy canes. Reluctantly, he pulled away and began closing the door.

"Can't wait till that next date."

The door shut on her unsatisfied and piqued face, leaving only shadows and glittering porch frost. He had to be quick. A hat of bone? A crown? What the literal fuck? Mimiko had to be hallucinating. That or some kind of fetish psycho lived in the forest. Deep in the arctic wilderness and away from the other kind of repressed Finns. No way in a freezing hell was strong but dim-as-a-fifteen-watt bulb Rocky behind this. He wasn't fast or smart enough. And why?

Kurt stepped from the stairs and a particularly bright flash of green illuminated the ground. He cautiously stalked onto the driveway of neon green, his boots *plodding* crunchy ice. It was surreal and dreamlike. His cold breath stuck in his throat, and a tingling sensation grazed his bare skin, the back of his neck, his face, the little patch of his throat with sprouting chest hairs. They tingled with the unmistakable fizz of an electrical charge. Or maybe it was just his nerves. Was an aurora strong enough to try and touch him on the ground? He almost wanted it to. To feel *that*.

Kurt closed his eyes, listening for a magnetic crackle overhead and instead heard another sound.

plodplodplodplodplodplodplodplodplod

His eyes shot open, discerning quick feet in snow, and he turned in the direction of the igloo trail. The sprinting feet halted all at once, the forest quiet, an unfamiliar and new stillness hung in the driveway. Motes of frost hung in the air before his eyes as if time had stopped and all waited on him.

Kurt inched hesitantly back for the lodge, a desire to see the owner of those feet stopping him on the bottom step, when a svelte snowman materialized from the trees thirty meters away. Kurt squinted. It raised a long black stick to its smooth and vague face, translucent breaths of steam blowing rapidly against the darkness. Kurt recognized too late what the stick really was, the motion of haint-arms drawing back, so unusual and out of place.

A beautiful, strange *whizzing* haunted the air, and the neckline of his shirt warmed, soaking down his shirtfront, the beginning of a tepid shower inside his clothes. Blood gurgled in the back of his throat like a broken faucet inside his body. It flowed everywhere, a gush, a flood, an overwhelming deluge forcing him to his knees. Kurt's brain, quickly losing blood, fired random synapses, sparks popping in odd sequences. A memory of his hand threading through curly hair, a hollowed reindeer hanging from a tree. The inside of the shed where he'd stored it. Flickering images connected links in a long chain, and he realized what was different about the shed. What was mostly missing.

He choked, gasping, a horrible gurgling sound, a death rattle and panic overtook his heart. A terrible fear that meshed the act of crying, sobbing, with fighting for air to breathe. He sobbed on his own blood. He didn't want to die. He wasn't ready. It was too late. He was alone.

A wide flash of light demanded his attention in the sky. It pulled him to here and now and his crying calmed. His back was oddly warm, then cold, his whole body cold except for the front of his shirt, and his eyes, tears frozen at the corners, blinked slowly at the aurora and arrow feathers filling his view. Like he was in front of an IMAX and a candescent movie played. It weaved streamers of emerald fire and pulsed like a great throbbing vein, and he wished he had gotten to know Carly more.

AINO

Kurt and Carly, an odd couple, kissed passionately at the door and Aino thought abruptly of Wilholm and his full red lips. How she would likely never taste them the way young lovers were meant to taste each other. With heat and smoke and fire smoldering your insides. And suddenly all her wise, careful choices abruptly turned into regrets. Something she never had, lost in an instant. She gave them their private moment and watched her father instead.

Mattias was leaning over his knees, sloppily mumbling in Lappish. A state she had never seen before. Confrontation, fighting, dealing with murder and death, didn't really seem in Mattias's wheelhouse. He hadn't fought the divorce. Nor the custody battle. Nor any disagreements with her grandfather. She could perfectly recall a fight between them and Mattias physically shrinking from her grizzled grandfather, his anger at some old feud unabated. The curmudgeon had died and their relationship remained eternally estranged.

Passive, jovial, round were the words usually used for Mattias. This half-crazed, incoherent, and despondent trainwreck was new.

Then again, so were two dead guests and a 'large, fast figure wearing a bone hat' in the woods. Aino's fears of bodily harm bizarrely quelled when her father curled up and became frustratingly useless.

"Boneandcrownboneandcrownboneandcrown," he murmured, the words slightly familiar. Where had he gotten the word 'crown' from? Like always, her gaze was drawn to her grandfather's painting.

She kneeled next to her father, "Mattias, let's get you into the bedroom."

His face was puffy from tears. "I never believed him."

She tugged on his forearms but he was planted as a dead weight in the chair. "I never believed him, Aino. I thought he was crazy. We all thought he was crazy."

He wasn't budging. She reached for his cup of tea, holding it to his lips. "Who was crazy?"

"Your grandfather."

He sipped the tea, liquid dribbling down his chin and through gray stubble.

"What are you talking about now? He *was* crazy. I mean towards the end, at least. Maybe even before I left. Remember how he used to make all those little figurines and plant them? The gnomes? Crazy." She tried to make him laugh, coax a smile. Something to bring him out of this and be helpful for once.

The front door shut and Mattias's stare lethargically roamed the remaining guests. Rocky stood at the hearth with a tense frame, hypnotized by the flames as if they held an answer. Carly leaned back against the front door and clenched the short and old rifle. And Mimiko, now silent, leaned her head down on the same table.

"*But what if he wasn't?*" Mattias's eyes widened frightfully, too large for his face. He whispered in Lappish and something about his voice and stare, similar to her grandfather's, roused an old, indistinct memory.

Aino frowned, Mattias neared a strange hysteria and if she was being honest, she was too, only doing a much better job of not letting it show. She had always taken care of him when he visited Helsinki. A daughter older than the flighty father. She was the responsible, sensible one. It was why she returned North to help. "Dad, let's go lay down. I think this Kurt–"

Mattias cut her off by abruptly grabbing her wrists, and the tea sloshed. His voice rose to a fevered and zealous pitch. "He always told me Aino, he always said I could never build on the land. It was my job, my responsibility to take care of it. If I didn't, grave things would happen. We argued, he ran my construction workers off, lost all that American money! Nearly had our family sued! Ruined my name for a decade! He never wavered and I always wondered why..."

"Dad, *you're* acting crazy. This is some psycho. The neighbor, Virtanen, you didn't see him, he was–"

"Aino!" he interjected, crazed. "It's the old gods, our *Haltija*. Our *luonto*."

Aino stared blankly at her father as he spoke of souls and animal deities.

"Right, I think we should get ready to move," Carly said at the door and everyone tensed. She held the gun across herself, strong and defiant as the metal, and Aino's body's internal alarm lessened a little with the sight. "Kurt will be back, hopefully only in a minute, then we're going to run to the barn. Aino, don't suppose you found those car keys, yeah?" She took a coat from the rack and approached Mimiko.

Aino stood. "No. I don't understand, I always leave them on the small rack, exactly so I *don't* lose them."

Mimiko pushed herself to stand, her limp much worse than before, and she pulled on the jacket before falling ungracefully onto the seat once more.

"I can hotwire a car," Rocky offered, approaching them. The women simply stared at him, and he shrugged. "I wasn't always a businessman."

Carly had assumed control of the small group and Aino was thankful for someone formidable and level-headed. Or maybe just experienced? Yes, Carly seemed to have experience; sure enough, she also studied Rocky cautiously. "Okay then, we'll take the two cars in that case. Better chance of..." Her words died as she looked to Aino and their stares met. Better chance of what?

Of surviving.

If there were two cars, one might get away.

Rocky, already dressed for outside, watched the one front window, parting the translucent curtains. "How do we get into the barn?"

Aino sniffled; she had thought the tears and bodily liquids had all been spent after Tetsuya. "The door shouldn't be locked, just turn the latch right and they slide open."

He nodded and flipped up the lapel of his jacket. His dark hair fell forward, and paired with his black eyes and strong features, the Texan held a dangerous and alluring quality. Carly hefted the rifle between her hands as if trying to test it without actually firing and nodded to a waiting Rocky. "Okay, I don't want to expose Mimiko's wound to the cold. By that limp, she's worse than I thought. We'll go start the cars and pull them in front of the steps, okay?"

Carly pointedly stared at Mattias, a maudlin mess, and the current liability in the group. The wildcard in movies that might suddenly open up the doors for a horde of zombies to rush in or the one to fall while everyone is running for dear life. Her stare then rose to meet Aino's. "Get him ready. Kurt should be back any minute." Then muttered, "He better be running that tight ass back here."

Rocky opened the door and they immediately turned right, their footsteps running along with the porch's wood to the end of the house. Aino glimpsed the green night as the door swung itself shut, then grabbed her father's coat.

"Let's get this on you, then come to the window. Revontulet is in the sky right now, it looks very strong." She said this with a hint of enthusiasm, hoping it stirred him to something. Anything.

Her father's head lifted with the word, a thoughtful expression. "Revontulet?" She nodded, physically threading his arm into the coat, and he allowed himself to be dressed as a child would. "Your grandfather always said..."

He shot up from the chair, the overwhelmed man gone, replaced with another frantic one, and went to the window. His round cheeks were laced with the spectral green of Revontulet and his lips moved without words, giving Aino more cause to worry.

But she moved to the table and Mimiko, who stared at the fire, her ungloved hands softly clasped and waiting in her lap. Even with her wound, she appeared at ease. Like the aftermath of turmoil and chaos was natural. She sighed, and Aino would have thought the expression beautiful had she not had smeared blood on her cheek. No, not that the chaos was natural, rather she was above it. Too good for such things. Aino frowned at her new calmness, remembering her sniveling state only fifteen minutes prior.

"Hiraki-san, was there anything you needed before we leave? How is your leg?"

Mimiko's head twisted, a sad, small smile on her lips. "It's fine. Just a 'flesh' wound, I think." She remained sitting and returned her attention to the fire.

Aino retrieved her own coat and stuck her gloves in the pocket, unsure if she would be asked to drive on the icy roads at night. Her father, still at the window, let the curtain drop, and a deep thought consumed his face. His brow scrunched and a trembling hand reached for his daughter and guided them both to the wall and a hanging print.

"Revontulet, Aino. I had forgotten."

Aino squeezed his hand. It was worn but clean, the crevices in his palm were deep. His tone was no longer upset. "Forgotten?"

He gestured to the picture with a dreamy, perhaps lost expression. It was a simple painting of the aurora over the sky, reflecting lake water, and a generic deity silhouetted black in the foreground. Something her grandfather painted?

"The lake, our family, Revontulet."

Back to speaking nonsense again. From his front chest pocket,

Aino plucked his beanie and covered his head. "What about the lake?" she asked, distracted. Where were his gloves? She patted his other pockets when he clutched both her hands to command her attention.

"We were stewards, first, Aino. That's what he always used to say. Hosts."

Aino frowned. 'Hosts?' The word made her insides shiver.

A great cry erupted from the front door and window. A howl of a tortured woman. The Australian. Aino left her father for the door just as it burst open, Rocky kicking it and dragging a body inside.

A short, crude arrow had struck at the bottom of Kurt's throat. His face and neck were blanched and milky blue, like the color of thick lake ice. Blood had streamed from the back of his throat where the arrow tip punched through but the drip was now frozen into a sharp splinter of metal and blood-ice. His wide-open mouth was frostbit at the edges of his cracked lips. Carly trailed the pair, the confident woman who had exchanged a warrior clasping a gun for a lamenting and broken maiden.

Her rifle clattered to the floor and she fell at Kurt's feet.

Aino simply stared at dead Kurt, awestricken and speechless. The arrow was short in length with old and grimy feathers. Rocky began talking over the crying Carly, a fast and jittery tone on his chapped lips.

"He was just at the front of the steps, just laying there, his blood was already starting to freeze into a pool."

As if in reflex, Aino reached into her pocket for her phone, pulling it out for the millionth time and checking the reception bars. Still none. She checked her messages, the failed exclamation sign beside her last attempted message to Wilholm. Nothing had gone through. She tapped the 'resend'. In the last two months since she'd arrived, the longest period without reception that she had noticed was three hours, tops. It had to open up again soon.

Aino rounded on her father, a new terrible fear rearing. Three bodies were beginning to tip the scales, soon there would be more dead than alive. "Mattias! Who is out there? It has to be that neighbor, yes? He is the only one I've ever heard of who lives this way. He lives off the land! He hunts with arrows and guns and knives, right?" What had he said to her earlier, in the van? Didn't he tell her to stay inside?

Mattias had resumed the vexing and unhelpful old-man role. His eyes were wide as he, too, stared down at the arrow lancinating Kurt's throat, its metal tip pushing his whole neck off the floor, his head falling back at an unsettling angle. Aino thought of the deer she'd gutted earlier.

Mattias stuttered:"I always thought he was lying, they were just stories, only stories! Who believes in *Haltija*? *Luonto*? No one, no one! He used to carve those little animals and gnomes and just throw them everywhere! They're stories!"

Aino wanted to smack him. For the first time in her life, she wanted to smack her father. Smack sense into him. Smack him for guilting her into returning after university. Smack him for marrying her mother. Smack him for living up here for her first twelve years so she felt a strange pull to the land, but not enough to make her stay. A child's nostalgia for a happy home. Enough to feel guilt, but not enough to act on it. Hurt him for not fighting for her. For not fighting for anything. She balled her hand into a fist and turned away.

"Let's get into the cars. We can bring him with us."

"We can't," Carly sniffled, her sobs spent, her face raw pink with freezer burn and glistening from frosty tears. She stared at the face of her dead boyfriend.

Rocky answered, his attention also on the arrow. "The tires of the cars were slashed."

"What?!" Aino hissed, her heart beating like a bird in a cage. Trapped. She was trapped here. Again.

"With something big. They were shredded, like with a machete. Someone doesn't want us leaving." Carly rose to stand over Kurt's corpse. She stared at him for a long second before turning to address the others. "The cars, the huskies, the reindeer. We would freeze if we tried for the main road. Someone doesn't want us to leave... alive."

She reached for the rifle once more and held it tight across her body, a defiant expression forming on her face stained with a short-lived grief. Aino sensed she had stiffened inside, reborn with Kurt's death.

"But..." her father suddenly spoke, and the group turned. "But those weren't the only reindeer."

"What? Where else do you keep reindeer?" Aino asked.

Mattias wiped his face down, as if he was brushing away the sniveling mess for his faculties to return. "There are... were, at least this afternoon, two males I tied by the river bridge. They were fighting earlier so I separated them from the herd and tied them up so maybe our guests would see them on the drive in."

A hopeful light came over his face, a welcome change. "I drove them by one sled each. They are beside the bridge."

Aino spoke her thoughts aloud: "Two reindeer and two sleighs, that's enough for four people, maybe five going slow back to the main road."

"If they're even still there," Mimiko spoke for the first time since the body came inside. Her small, innocuous voice was firm and rather calm. Factual.

Carly sniffled, no longer hurt or sad but rather unphased by this new obstacle. Like all the surprise had been drained out of her, and only sheer will now propped her up. Sheer will of someone bigger than her body. Aino had never wanted to be someone else so much in her entire life.

"They're still there. They have to be. I'm not going to die in some fucking frozen forest." Carly tossed the rifle five feet across to Aino, who surprised herself more than anyone by catching it and then holding it firm. With a determined stride, Carly stepped over Kurt's body and made for the kitchen, appearing a second later with a large chef's knife. Hefty and thick.

"Okay, I think we have determined staying in the house is safest.

Leaving alone is not smart. So Mattias leads Rocky and me to the reindeer, we get them ready and ride back to—"

"I'm not going out there," Rocky abruptly cut in.

The four others stared at him, and his glare nervously twitched between each of them and then to the body on the floor.

Carly gritted through her teeth, "I need someone to watch my ba—"

"You're goddamn crazy going out there. Not when..." His mouth clamped down on the last two words, his face turning passive at sight of the arrow.

Aino picked up on his mistake. "Not when... what? What do you know?" she demanded. How could he know anything? He was a visitor. Here for less than ten hours. But this all had happened as the guests arrived. Their presence had started something.

Or they'd brought something with them.

He covered his reticence poorly, like a lying salesman caught in his scam. "Not when there is something out there with a fucking bow and arrow and some kind of machete. Who the fuck uses a machete?!"

Carly inhaled and exhaled a deep breath. Aino guessed she wanted to save her strength for the elements and any more surprises... or arrows. Not for fighting with a man-child like Rocky. "Fine, then you can move Kurt's body." She gestured at the gun. "You know how to use that thing?"

Aino stared at the rifle, large in her small hands, old chrome reflecting her heart-shaped face in odd, lanky distortions. A sicker, mutated Aino watched her from the gun. Judging her. She tilted the receiver up, the safety switch on, and fingered it to show she knew. She was her grandfather's progeny, after all. He used traps, but the gun had always been there, well cared for.

The slightly older woman nodded, satisfied, and moved for the door. "Okay, Mattias looks like it's only you and I. Brave face, yeah?"

Mattias timidly stepped forward, his body twitching and stretching, and Aino had the distinct notion he was being served on a platter for a foreigner. Like exotic reindeer meat for them to 'ooooh' and 'ahhh' as they tasted with fat lips and sharp teeth. She abruptly clutched his shoulder. Three out of eight dead. No rhyme or reason as to who or why. Her throat tightened.

"Dad, be... I don't know. Be careful. Stick to the trees, yes?"

His eyes glinted wet in the firelight and his mouth turned up at one corner to speak in Finnish. He spoke with a new surety that had arisen from parts unknown in the last two minutes, as if a puzzle piece clicked in his mind–the picture, the ending, laid bare for only him to foresee. "Don't worry, dearheart. We're of the land. Our *Haltija* is the spirit that protects the land, our property, us. It won't hurt me, dearheart. Not under Revontulet. Especially not."

He said it so matter-of-factly that it left Aino confused. Her mouth hung open and his eyes lowered to it expectantly, waiting for her to say something.

Tell him you love him, she thought. An urgent, looming desire born of fear, more regrets, told her to say everything she felt but had never expressed with the gift of words. *Just one 'I love you'.* She never had the time or inclination to say it often, because he had just... let her go. He let them leave. She frowned, and he looked at that too.

He succinctly nodded, as if that was that, the end, and exited the doorway with Carly, holding the knife like an extension of her hand. Her gaze flicked between Rocky at the fireplace, now awkwardly chewing his nails, and Mimiko, sitting erect at the table and camply watching them leave.

"You just hold that gun tight, okay?" Carly said.

Aino nodded, the cold steel in her palms, the pulse of her blood pushing against it. Her mouth opened like she wanted to say something final to Mattias, her father, but they had already opened the door. The breeze had died again and the anticipated hush of an arctic night seeped through the doorway. Her father left without another word.

MATTIAS

Aino's lips pursed together and Mattias saw her mother, his ex-wife, in her face more acutely than ever. In her smile. Her eyes were her grandfather's but her mouth was his ex-wife's. Why did he let them leave all those years ago? His daughter's lips then turned into a particularly grizzly frown, also resembling her mother, and then the door closed between them and Mattias was in the cold. Ah, yes, because his wife was unhappy. Because he made her unhappy. All his failures had made them miserable and she had fervently wanted to leave him for more exciting places. He nodded to his beautiful daughter behind the door and left.

As soon as the door shut and the warmth departed, the ambient light of the Revontulet was all Mattias knew as his eyes adjusted. Carly strode in front of him and down the steps, each tread alert and slow, a mimicry of a wary cat. She didn't look up at the phenomena as anyone else would; instead her gaze had zeroed in on the treeline, bathed in reflecting snow and slivers of darkness. Once the two were off the steps, her arm reached out, holding him back. He stepped aside, and his boot unexpectedly squished in near-frozen liquid.

He looked down, puzzled to see a pool of black tar, a small trickle coursing down the slight incline of the driveway, its source a mystery until his boot squished again in the smear of gradual blood leading back to the lodge. He quickly stepped out of Kurt's lifeblood, staring in dread at the liters stained like ink on a white blanket. Carly looked back at his sudden movement, following his gaze.

He had the terrifying sensation she might cry again, similar to the weeping mess he had been for the last hour. Revert to a more natural state of being after everything. It was natural to cry, abnormal if one did not. Everything happened so fast. Dizzying speeds. The night, the deaths. It all began with the Revontulet. Mischievous spirits, all set into motion when Mattias, his father's traitor, brought foreigners here and harbored designs for raping their ancestral land.

"I'm sorry," he said, though it seemed a ridiculous thing to say at that moment. Or was he saying it aloud for the spirits, to his father, himself?

But Carly seemed to understand it only for her. She sniffed against the frost-bitten air. "We weren't dating for very long," she said with indifference. Gesturing ahead, she asked, "Which way?"

He stepped wide, over the blood creek, and together they walked down the driveway, their boots the loudest thing Mattias ever imagined. In the open air, he felt like an animal in a cage he couldn't see. Watched and toyed with. The open space had become hostile. He pointed around the curve of the drive, a white, bioluminescent snake lost to the forest on either side. "The bridge where I tied them is five minutes away. You drove over it when you came in, though you wouldn't have noticed because the river is mostly frozen over."

She grabbed his upper arm, pulling him with unexpected strength, and he didn't resist as Carly led him into the dense trees. Beneath the ceiling of branches and needles, the snow-laden ground glittered smooth. Occasionally there was the blemish of a fallen pack of snow from a branch above, but they were few. The forest slept for winter, the snow promising an intimate silence in the forest, assuring rest.

Mattias led the way, keeping the road on his right and two or three trees apart. He idly wondered what the Järvinen family *Haltiji*, their protector, would appear as. A wolverine? No, the Japanese woman said bones. A reindeer? Or maybe it was not even the family's personal protector at all.

Maybe it was a God.

Mielikki, Goddess of the forest and the hunt. But she was a healer, creator of the Bear. Yes, she carried a bow, but why? Why would she hurt them? He now wasn't as sure that he and Aino were beyond suffering.

His foot sank into a snow-filled hole, and Mattias's ankle tweaked, a sharp stab of pain that was gone a second later. More of an irritation, really.

Lempo.

It could be the God, Lempo. Once the goddess of love and fertility, her spirit became reckless, and now was a wild, erratic soul of the wilderness. Commander of demons. Yes, yes, she also used a bow. It would make much more sense. A mischievous spirit. He weaved around a wide pine, ducking for its low branches, and listened to their steps, their breaths, the only sound in the winter hush.

"You've lived here all your life?" Carly asked, her voice low and only slightly strained with exercise unlike his own heavy breath.

"Yes. No. As a child, yes, my father and I. But I found Aino's mother young and married young. We lived in the town about two hours south."

"And your dad stayed here, by himself? No other family or people living close by?"

Carly hoped to figure out who had killed the other guest. Mattias couldn't tell her about Lempo or Mielikki or the family *Haltiji*. The part of their soul, *luonto*. Foreigners with their modern ways wouldn't understand. He hadn't understood. He hadn't even listened to his father's rambling. His *truths*.

"Yes, he was alone. Aino and I would visit him every weekend and camp in the forest or kayak in the lake. He and Aino would take long walks, rides. Sometimes. They were close." His throat closed at the memory of little Aino catching her first fish and her grandfather hugging her, the folds of his old skin squishing together. Her smile with baby teeth burned in his memory. "Though we disagreed, there were some good times. It is a special forest. A special place."

"Mmmmm. How did he die?" she asked, searching for answers. Sieving for clues.

He brushed a low branch aside, heavy with snow that *plonked* to the ground. "Nothing like this. He was just old. He was by…" The image Mattias would never forget came unbidden. "I found him by the lakeside, a fishing pole in his hand." His whispered voice was barely audible. "It seemed peaceful. He was just sitting there… eyes closed. Even had his bare feet in the water, like he would float away."

The visual of his father's back, sitting in a deck chair at the water's edge, the midnight sun splaying prismatic golden light. Mattias knew the old man died happy. Or at least naturally. He imagined his soul drifted, flowed into the lake, and there was nothing more natural than that.

Carly stepped in his tread, making her hike easier than his own, so she spoke with less hardship. "Sounds like a nice way to go. Sounds lucky."

His gloved hand gripped the body of a rough pine, hoar-frosted for winter. "Nothing is lucky here. These woods, they're old, carved from the ice. These trees earned their roots, drunk from the deepest wells of the glaciers, where frozen things survived." Bone and crown. Nothing was a coincidence when everything fought to survive. It was designed.

He was rambling, an eerie echo of his late father. Ideas strung together in words until they made an image. A mosaic of broken pieces creating something larger. But Carly listened, her breath pacing itself steadily like she was practiced at extreme exercise. The trees grew lighter and eventually less dense and a tinkle of a bell rang ahead. Mattias wove around another tree. Some fifteen meters away, they ended at the river, running through the land as a giant serpent heading for the frozen Bering Sea.

Shadows moved and the silhouettes of the two reindeer were exposed against the ambient night–murky, spindly shadows skirting the ocean of lime-snow ground. They raised their heads with the crunch of his footsteps, festive bells at their necks jingling. A sweet sound reminded Mattias of all the happy winters here. Beyond them stood the rotting wood railing of the bridge, layered in last night's snowfall, as well as the outline of two low sitting sleighs. Carly's hand gripped his shoulder.

"Wait. Think."

He stopped, the reindeer sensing their presence with twitching ears. Innocuously waiting, the trees silent, the breeze dead. Carly readjusted the knife in her free hand and licked her dry lips. Mattias resisted the urge to tell her not to, that water on the skin was no good in -15 air, it would quietly put a layer of frost on her skin.

She fidgeted from foot to foot and whispered quickly. "Look, as soon as we leave the trees, we're exposed. So we have to be fast. The reindeer know you and I don't know shit about hooking up a sleigh."

He nodded and watched them as she thought aloud. Their heads abruptly flicked the opposite way, to the river, and he wondered how fast the water moved tonight.

"We're going to pull both reindeer at the same time over to their sleighs." She licked her lips again, a flash of pink on white skin, her words faster as she psyched herself up. "Okayokayokay, line them next to each other and stay between them while you hook them up. Understand? Use their bodies as cover, got it?"

A branch cracked in the distance, snow thudding like a body hitting a mattress, and the pair stood still. Waiting for further movement. The tread of something old or new.

When there was nothing, Carly's tense shoulders beneath her thick jacket relaxed and she motioned forward. The reindeer stomped and tugged at the short ropes fettering them to the pines. They only stopped pulling when Mattias revealed himself from the gloom. They didn't know him so well. They were his father's reindeer, his children of a sort. Every reindeer in Finland belonged to someone, and these and their offspring had been with the Järvinens longer than memory. But his father had been the one who loved them, exercised them on daily rides, making his own sleigh tracks coursing through the land like secret little veins. They probably knew this land better than Mattias.

Carly untied the left one first and then the right, their hot snorts clouding the air in erratic bursts. "Okay boy, okay Toivo, it's okay," Mattias whispered, leading them to the bridge.

The river surface, some fifteen meters wide, was mostly frozen, snowdrift and ice layering it shades of white and gray. Thin ice. It was completely covered except for a thin, foot-wide sliver down the middle. A black stripe of death, dark water, fast and rebellious. It barreled away to the lake, ice occasionally cracking against its force. He heaved the first reindeer–Leevi, a large old male–against the railing, the wood creaking as its hefty body knocked against it.

Carly was suddenly beside him with the second, Toivo, guiding the beast with a skilled hand familiar with animals. Her head swiveled, scanning everywhere at once, tension rolling off her in palpable waves. "This outside one first," she commanded, and Mattias turned to the reindeer. A younger, smaller male, Toivo wasn't yet well trained for the sleigh and somewhat unfamiliar with commands. He would always run when sometimes a nice slow ride was needed. But he was strong.

He crouched, reaching under for the hanging strap. The reindeer's smooth belly rose and fell and only slightly flinched as Mattias pulled the sled bars beside his haunches and strapped him into the harness. Carly crooned softly to the older Leevi, stroking his neck as she pressed close to him, stuck between the two. Mattias exhaled shakily, listening to her kind tones, hearing a familiar tenderness in them his father often used, and he pushed the words out.

"If I..." Carly continued caressing the bull but gave Mattias her attention. "If I don't... please help Aino. She never wanted to be here. She was only helping an old man. Please help her get out."

Carly's hand paused on the reindeer's neck and she smirked, an odd gesture on a cold, dark bridge. "How do you know I'm not the one doing all this?"

He stared pointedly at her hand stroking the deer. He didn't want to mention any of his thoughts about what *was* doing this, but clearly someone who calmed a reindeer with soothing words most likely wouldn't kill anyone. She looked to her hand, catching his meaning, and scratched the fur. "Okay, old-timer. I'll do my best. Save the daughter. No worries."

He nodded, inexplicably relieved, and cinched the last buckle across Toivo's low chest, affectionately rubbing its neck, when the reindeer's head flinched, startled by something.

Rising to crouch, Mattias peeked over the reindeer's back, viewing nothing but the white snow of the driveway leading through the forest to the main road. But then the very snow moved right before his eyes, white on white shifting, and a strange *whip* scored the air. An arrow abruptly appeared in Toivo's hind flank and the animal brayed, immediately bolting. Its chest knocked Mattias to the ground and the connected sleigh ran over his whole body as the panicked reindeer tore away and back to the house with the frantic jingle of a bell.

Less than a second later, a blink, another *whip* sailed over the bridge, and the second reindeer cried a painful belt outmatched by Carly's raw scream.

From the ground where he lay, Mattias rolled, his leg broken, and witnessed an arrow piercing through the back of Carly's shoulder and into the reindeer she had been hugging. The arrow's feathers were near to her coat, meaning the arrow head punched deep into the reindeer's neck. The two were locked, prisoners of the same shaft.

Leevi the reindeer attempted rearing on his hind legs, but Carly and her new, unfamiliar weight toppled him sidewards. The wood railing cracked beneath them and all at once broke with a snap. The reindeer fell over the side, Carly dragged with him by the arrow piercing them both.

They toppled into the river, out of Mattias's sight, and Carly's shriek was replaced with snapping ice and the muffled splash of hungry arctic water devouring them. On elbows and knees, he scrambled to the bridge's edge, only to find a large black hole in the middle of the narrow strip where the two had dropped in, pulled under the ice flowing to the sacred lake.

Mattias exhaled. It all happened in five seconds, no more. He inhaled and a fierce, driving pain in his chest made him roll to his back. Something inside his old body was also impaled, he could feel it as sure as he could feel he was at fault for all of this. An innate knowledge. A genetic guilt.

He stared overhead, rivers of green light coursing through the sky, mirroring the black one below, and in his lower periphery, the snow ran to him. *Plodplodplodplod.* A white figure rushed to the remaining railing, examining below, then smacked its hands on the wood in a very human-like manner of frustration.

"You're not my *Haltaji*," he murmured. He was benumbed. Beyond cold. Mattias was once indifferent to the cold. He grew up in the North. The frozen North. The North that made vikings hard. He might have been a failure as a husband and man, always scrambling for money, a living, always thinking up the next scheme, but his body should have been immune to the cold. This cold was different. Final. He couldn't hold his head up anymore and let it fall to the soft snow. The Revontulet above swelled in pulses, like new water after years of drought, waters slowly and surely creating a new course.

Strong hands tugged his shoulders, yanking his whole limp body until his head partially hung off the side of the bridge, and something sharp stabbed the soft, fatty folds of his neck. A blade of fire dug inside him. More agony erupted and hot blood trickled off the back of his nape. He tried to scream but those muscles didn't obey him anymore and remained slack. Cut.

A hand, ungloved, clawed his scalp and lifted it to meet his eyes.

Lempo. Angry, vengeful God of wilderness stared at him. Those eyes were feral and wild. Cursed. Reminding him of all the bad things he had done in his life. Not terrible, but not right. Did anyone try to be terrible in this short life?

Blood left his body, life falling into the pitch water beneath, and something stirred in his memory as the cold seeped up from his booted toes. A story of his father's and the lake. His father had taken his final sleep in the lake. Cold crawled up his legs with icicles for fingers. Something about sacrifice, his family, their blood, his blood. The devastating chill curled his guts and dinner solid, a hefty weight sitting in his body like a large stone. A story of the lake and the forest and his family and their duty and their protection and their custodianship over sacred land that should never be taken or stolen or used ill. His chest with its broken organ slowed and Mattias stared dreamily at the Revontulet, a flare of red unexpectedly surging through the green. He was dreaming.

Mattias no longer felt his legs or body but had the distinct sensation of vertigo as Lempo lifted his two heavy feet and he fell through frigid air to frozen water. He choked the terrible, numbing water, surprised when he discovered his body, nearly devoid of life, floated.

Ushered down the fast-moving river, ice cut his body, though he didn't notice much as he was transfixed by the celestial light. The water rumbled, the river bed churned, and sound and movement shuddered everything everywhere all at once, and Mattias could only lax into numbness. Above, emerald, lush and wild, clashed with primal vermillion. The colors enameled the sky in broad strokes, guiding his way. They showed him the path, and faces took shape within the Revontulet. Beautiful, terrible faces. Horrific, familiar faces. Bears, wolverines, foxes, reindeer, wolves, lynx, seals. Figures of lore, ancient, terrible deities floating in the sky, in the gateway to heaven or hell, waiting to take him into the dark memories of his lineage.

AINO

Mattias and Carly walked to the treeline opposite the driveway as stealthily as possible. In Mattias's mind, this seemed to mean slumping his shoulders, bending his head little, and his knees not at all. The Australian woman, however, moved like a lithe spider, melding into the scenery, her younger years and agile limbs a stark contrast to the old man.

Aino sucked in a fortifying breath as they faded away. If the killer outside followed, most likely only Carly would survive. The old and weak were first to die in the wild. Nature's finest fuck you for beating the odds for so long.

She had sudden remorse at being so bitter against Mattias, her father, and she stared at the spot where they disappeared for a long moment. The forest across from the house stood solemn. In the cold night and after so much madness, Aino looked at it with new understanding. Elegant trees were cast in winter beauty, glittering in a ghostly light. Who wouldn't love to stay here, in the wild North? It was beauty and life, made more magnificent for the hardships it endured. The world was hard, the North prevailed.

The curtain dropped and she turned to the others. The other

survivors.

Mimiko continued sitting at the table. The gauze and small towel around her leg were still clean, meaning her wound must have bled only a little. She appeared tired but more than that, wary.

And she stared right at Rocky.

Still beside the fire, orange flickering light bathed him in sinister hues. His fingers drummed relentlessly on the wooden mantel, staring into the flames with glazed eyes and a foot that jiggled on its ball with nervous energy. Aino watched him, slowly walking to the other end of the table with as much casualness as she could muster, trying to escape his notice. The gun was heavy and unfamiliar. She had only fired it once many years ago—a practice shot that went way off target, and her grandfather snatched it from her trembling hands, mumbling curses while she tried not to cry in front of him.

An animal howled outside, maybe an escaped husky or maybe only the wind, and Aino realized they were readying for a flight or fight dash. A panic-ridden sleigh ride through the gloom. Through polar midnight. It would be another world of cold. An alien and hostile blight.

"I..." Mimiko and Rocky turned at the sound of her unsure voice, "I'm going to get some thermoses ready." Rocky frowned at her. "For the trip, you know. Going to be bitter out there."

She made for the kitchen when Mimiko shot up from her seat, the wooden chair scraping along the floor. "I'll help you," she said.

After a long, tense moment, Aino nodded. "Sure."

Both women turned their backs on Rocky, and Aino's scalp tingled, knowing he was watching them leave. The kitchen had been cleaned since dinner, the dishwasher ready for unloading. Aino opened the new cupboards, scents of fresh pine still lingering. The whole kitchen had been upgraded since her father moved into her grandfather's old and traditional lodge and renovated most of it. How the bathroom was left for last, Aino didn't understand, but she guessed Mattias had run out of money. He had never been good with money, if her mother's stories were true.

Three large chrome thermoses waited, bought for guest tours. Reindeer-drawn sleigh rides in soft-falling snow, panoramas of lakes and Santa villages, with magical hidden grottos waiting for foreigners to discover their secrets while sipping hot cocoa. Now they would be used for survival against frostbite and hypothermia. Aino's belly suddenly felt empty.

Mimiko spotted the kettle and filled it with water, placing it atop the gas stove while Aino found the tea bags, watching the other woman out of the corner of her eye. She was so small, petite, and Aino swore she trembled ever so slightly, hiding her face with a lock of fallen fringe, her black hair thick and full.

Aino cursed at herself. Of course, Mimiko was on the brink and shaking. She had lost her husband *and* her friend in the space of an hour. Aino only had her mother and father, and he had literally been a country away for the last decade. She didn't know what level of grief she would experience when—if—Mattias did not return.

Mimiko continued simply standing beside the stove with erect shoulders and spine, her posture something cryptic and inarticulable. A softness and grace that transcended such words. Aino's immediate thoughts went to some kind of finishing school, an image of a lady with a book on her head.

"I'm sorry about your husband."

Mimiko's head turned ever so slightly before resuming her watch over the kettle. "He wasn't the best husband or even man." Aino watched her reflection in the kettle. Just like the chrome gun, the reflection showed a distorted creature with glazed, dead eyes. Mourning eyes. "He did some bad things and sometimes wasn't bad enough."

Aino paused her hand reaching for the tea box, the reflection now fogged as the kettle grew hot. She didn't reply. What a strange thing to say. A husband who wasn't bad enough? Was that some kind of Japanese thing she didn't understand?

Rocky's heavy footsteps walked across the main room, maybe to the front window, drawing both's attention.

"But at least he loved me," Mimiko whispered.

The kettle started steaming and Aino stepped in toward the other woman. "Who did you see outside?"

Mimiko's soft pink lips parted only to shut, and her stare moved to the open, empty doorway. She didn't want to name him—a goliath in comparison to both women, and they were alone. Well, alone with a gun.

Instead of admitting it, Mimiko leaned in and whispered, "He's not a good man, either. He used to hurt her, steal from her. I think he had something to do with her father's death."

Worry creased Aino's brow, as she remembered Regina's bruise and the awkward wrist-grabbing scene. She wished Carly had returned already, or rather that they had all left together. Why hadn't she insisted on that? The Australian woman seemed like she had no fear, certainly not against a stronger, angry man like Rocky Armstrong.

"I can't remember where he was when my husband..." Mimiko's jaw clenched and she couldn't force the words out. When her husband was murdered. Aino couldn't remember either. Tetsuya had left for the igloo and was gone for a while before they found him. Everyone had been inside, though Aino knew Rocky left at least once to use the outhouse.

"I think he was outside at one time," she whispered. Mimiko's eyes welled, and her lips pursed together in a tight scrunch, holding something in.

The kettle sang a high-pitched tune, a soprano's whistle, and Mimiko lifted it. She held the large and heavy kettle easily, pouring with such a unique delicacy. Aino was mesmerized. Mimiko's wrist strained, showing a hidden strength, but she remained graceful. A glimpse of color revealed a tattoo on her wrist, and Aino's bewitchment broke as she blinked at the odd feature for such an elegant woman. Antithetical to what she would have thought for a sophisticated Japanese woman.

Aino screwed the lids as Mimiko finished pouring one container and moved to the next. She was about to ask Mimiko if her style of pouring was a Japanese thing, a tea ceremony perhaps, when her jacket pocket vibrated with her phone.

"Ladies," Rocky said, startling both women.

He raised his hands as if apologizing for his abruptness without actually doing so.

Aino screwed on the top of the thermos, avoiding his stare in case he should see something accusatory she didn't like. Lowering her eyes like you would an angry animal. Hugging the three thermoses in her arms, she placed them in a small satchel bag from under the sink.

"Yes?"

She made to leave the kitchen and he stepped away, unblocking the door. "This is awkward but I gotta use the bathroom." His stomach quite clearly gurgled.

"Um, okay. You remember where it is?" She gestured to the back door.

He followed her gaze, nodding. "Yeahhhh, I don't.." He looked back at the women, and for the first time, he seemed nervous. "Can one of y'all come outside with me?" They glanced at each other, their thoughts obvious. Mimiko's nose scrunched in clear distaste. "I hate to ask but I get a real funny tummy when I'm stressed. Will only take a minute, likely two."

No fucking way Aino would go outside alone with that man. She felt a foreboding in her stomach that he would kill her with one of those giant fists. So simple for him to just hit her in the head and that would be the end of that.

Mimiko and Aino glanced at each other and he caught their apprehension. "I just... it's not safe to go anywhere alone, right?"

His stomach gurgled louder.

"Yes, of course, you're right. We'll leave the door open to the back. I don't think she should be outside needlessly," Aino said, gesturing to Mimiko.

Rocky's mouth opened for an argument only to shut again. "All right then, best I can ask for."

He left for the door and the women followed slowly, Mimiko's limp not nearly as bad now. As the door opened, the frigid, heavy air of the yard met them. The floodlight illuminated the clear space all the way to the treeline, making the red ice of Regina's death glisten. It was so quiet. They stalled at the doorway, breathing in the frosty air, sacrificing the warm one behind them. The feel of the night reminded Aino of the sky before a heavy snowfall–the indescribable, full quality in the atmosphere until pregnant clouds birthed curtains of snow. But the sky was full of Revontulet, not clouds.

It troubled her, and she wanted nothing more than to shut the door and leave him outside.

"Fuck," Rocky said, undoubtedly also feeling the tension and strained atmosphere. They were on the precipice of something inescapable. Like they had dived off a seaside cliff and couldn't escape the water below. But then he knuckled his side and scooted outside. "Hell with it," he muttered, nearly running for the end of the porch.

Out of their line of sight, the bathroom door slammed shut, and the loud lock turned. The women both leaned on either side of the doorframe, Mimiko wincing, repositioning her leg more comfortably, and she shivered, the spasm running down her body.

Aino studied her calf. Whatever had cut her had also made short work of the snow pants material, cutting it away like silk. Beneath the gauze and towel was her bare open wound. Not good for traveling.

"You know, I'm going to get you extra clothes. You'll freeze before we get anywhere."

Mimiko simply nodded, and Aino left her in the open doorway. She unexpectedly followed and the door closed by itself. Aino paused, concerned, but the other woman waved a hand. "Don't worry, that man always takes care of himself. He'll be fine."

Aino grimaced but continued to her room, the first in the short corridor and right beside the open living room. Her clothes were folded neatly in drawers, and she laid the rifle on the bed. Mimiko needed clothes slightly bigger so they'd fit over her existing clothes. The silence in the house was now palpable, needing to be filled.

"You and the American woman were... great friends?" It was the nicest, most polite thing Aino could think of discussing. It hadn't escaped her notice that Mimiko cried and wailed over Regina's death more than her frozen husband's.

"He was always jealous of her," Mimiko murmured, and Aino stopped rifling through her pants. Mimiko stared through the lodge at the back door. Did she mean Rocky was jealous of his wife?

"She had so many dreams, she was going to be great, going to do great things. Then her father lost most of her inheritance and suddenly Rocky was there. They married before I even knew his name." Mimiko turned her profile away from Aino and she spoke somberly. "They wouldn't let us visit."

It was the most Mimiko had uttered since arriving, and she spoke as if recalling a terrible nightmare she couldn't forget and would never escape. Aino found the pants and jacket she intended to wrap over the delicate woman and handed them to her, shaking them to draw her from her mournful thoughts.

Mimiko wiped her face and an unseen tear beneath her eye, accepting the clothes with an embarrassed grin. "She was so smart. That's what I liked about her. She was so intelligent and never tried to prove otherwise. She didn't care what others thought of her. That's real power, having it and not flaunting it."

Mimiko wandered into the main room, placing the new clothes on the chair by the fire, still in her dream. Aino followed, the shotgun back in her hand. Her unkind thoughts about 'ski-bunny,' stereotypical airhead Regina returned to shame her. She was so quick to judge and never thought twice. How many others did she not think twice over?

"He was always so jealous..." Mimiko mumbled.

A vibration trembled Aino's chest as the other woman stared into the fireplace, and Aino recalled her phone vibrating earlier.

But the vibration grew, and it wasn't from her pocket.

It came from her chest, the very center, the core of her body. Her essence. A vibration growing into a flutter, then a tremble, then a shake, then a great spasm of her entire frame. A terrible convulsion, a distant thunder rattling with spindly numbing, blinding cold. Her blood trembled on an atomic level. Writhing everywhere, it forced Aino onto her knees, gasping for breath like she was trapped beneath the frozen lake. Her fingernails clawed the wood floor, the ice above, the world rolling her over, digging splinters beneath her nails.

"Aino?" Mimiko kneeled beside her, a warm hand on her neck.

Her body stopped seizing all at once. Like a switch had been flicked inside and she blinked at the floor. She rested on all fours, Mimiko kneeling, helpless and confused. She pushed up to her knees, breath returning to her constricted lungs.

"Did you... feel that?"

Mimiko shook her head, her brow creased. "There was nothing, you were having a fit. Have you had one before?"

A coldness curdled Aino's insides, her thoughts flying down the road to her father. Shouldn't they have been back by now? They'd been gone for ten minutes, easily. Drool had run down her chin, and Aino wiped it away "No, I have never had one before. I... I don't know. At first, I thought it was my phone..."

She remembered the small vibration in her pocket earlier in the kitchen. "My phone buzzed before!" she exclaimed, hope rising as her hand scrambled to open the zipped pocket. The phone woke at her touch, and a message from Wilholm popped onto the screen. Her last text, the one she tried to resend, had gone through at some stage.

Call the police. The Japanese man has been murdered, get them to come out to the property! ASAP.

His replies arrived ten minutes earlier.

What? Are you serious or is this a ploy to get me out there?

Aino? Are you serious?

One bar rested at the top of her screen and she tapped to reply 'Yes, she was fucking serious' when footsteps stumbled over wood and running water splashed loudly outside. Mimiko, who'd been watching her with the phone, flinched at the abrupt sound, and both studied the back door. Aino's rifle lay forgotten on the floor and Mimiko picked it up slowly, the reply to Wilholm momentarily forgotten.

Rocky was outside.

Aino followed Mimiko, who'd somehow become the new leader with a hidden reserve of courage. She reached for the door handle, flinging it open wide and stepped outside. On the side of the house, Rocky used the outdoor faucet. And his legs were drenched in dark blood.

His gloved hands swiped water onto the parts of his legs that freely dripped gore, a poor attempt to clean himself and hide evidence, and his head whipped to the women across the yard, surprised at being caught.

"This isn't what it looks like."

Mimiko immediately raised the shotgun, holding it expertly. "Stop talking!"

Rocky's translucent-red, wet hands flung up in surrender. "Jesus! It's not what it looks like!"

Aino's stomach churned at the sight of the blood; like he had been finger painting in it. But you couldn't replicate blood with paint. The texture was too...syrupy. She thought of the calf she'd skinned earlier. The color was too vivid.

Her cheeks became coated with saliva, warning that she might vomit again. "Whooo..whose blood is that?"

His mouth opened to answer only for Mimiko to interrupt, "What did you do to them?"

Aino blinked. Her father. Carly. They were running late. But Rocky had only been outside for no more than five minutes. His hand dripped with the concoction of water and blood. Five minutes would be enough. Wouldn't it? Life could change in moments. Car accidents happened in seconds, a heart attack in a minute. Life was long but death was quick. Tears threatened her eyes, the stinging sensation of salt on raw, tired eyeballs.

"I...I...I haven't done anything to anyone, I went into—"

"*Don't lie,*" Aino gritted through her teeth. A smudge of blood had caught beneath his chin, ruining his devilish, handsome face. She wanted to scream at him, make a show, threaten him and intimidate him although she was only a 5'3" twenty-two year old and he was a large, wrathful, murderer.

He walked forward, slowly, hands still raised. Ignoring Mimiko with the gun, he focused on her. "Aino, there has been some mistake." He stepped up the first porch stair. Then the second. "I don't know what's going on here tonight but..."

Mimiko stepped forward, pressing the rifle's sharp metal into his cheek. "Did you kill my husband?"

"Mimiko, you know I didn't do..."

She rounded on him quickly and prodded the barrel into his shoulder. "Inside. Get inside." Her voice trembled, the hurt of thinking her friend murdered by her husband unmistakeable. Aino backed up for him, her body tense and on edge like a tightened spring.

Rocky's face was alert but not aggressive, and he pleaded only with Aino. "Aino, I think something is happening, I went to see my wife's body, to see Tetsuya's body in the shed..."

Mimiko's gun jabbed harder, pushing him forward. "You'll never touch her again. Now sit." He didn't move at first, and she stabbed the gun into his collarbone. "*Sit!*" she commanded.

The new fire in Mimiko's voice was a welcome confidence. Without Carly, someone needed to handle this man, hold the gun to him.

Rocky strode slowly to the chair and calmly sat, the women in front of him and the rifle still cocked onto Mimiko's shoulder like it belonged there.

"Aino... did you say your phone was working?"

She blinked, "Yes! Yes!" She retrieved it from her pocket.

"Okay, call your friend. Tell him it's Rocky Armstrong. Tell him to send help."

She bit off her gloves and pressed dial. Rocky began talking as the ringtone began, sporadically breaking into crackling static.

"Aino, I went to see my wife. And there was a tub of blood, nearly half empty, in the shed. I tripped over it."

The dial ended and Wilholm's deep voice came through, scratchy and far from her.

"*Aino? Are you serious? Are you okay?*" His words came out broken through the connection.

"Wilholm! Call the police, the American man, Armstrong, he killed my father. The others..."

Wilholm's response cut off mid-word, crackling consuming his voice until the electrical distortion from the Revontulet strangely howled at her before clicking off. Aino stared at the phone's screen just as it disconnected, the bar fluttered like a dying moth.

"Did he hear you?" Mimiko asked, simultaneously nervous and hopeful.

"I think so. I'll try again."

Rocky shook his head calmly, his weight resting in the chair casually as if he wasn't the prisoner at all. "Aino, she wasn't in the shed."

"What do you think he'll do? Will he call the police?" Mimiko asked, and Aino's brain stalled at the two statements. No body in the shed? But she answered Mimiko.

"Yes, he'll call, we have to hold him for about two hours though."

Mimiko sighed. "Well, we better hurry then."

Aino turned in time for the butt end of the rifle her grandfather had used to hunt grouse to strike perfectly against her forehead.

ROCKY

Aino dropped to the floor like a sack of potatoes and Rocky winced for her. The gun's buttress left an immediate red mark on her unconscious face, and he'd bet by night's end it would be black and blue.

If she was still alive.

He doubted it.

Mimiko stood over her, her frame stiff and unyielding, still pointing the rifle carelessly his way, not bothering to even look at him. Her whole demeanor had changed in a flash. Scared anger turned into confidence, the minute tremors of her hands and voice gone. All a performance. The rattlesnake sloughing its old dry husk.

"Fucking Geishas," he mumbled. Their stares met, hers nearly indifferent. "Goddamn prostitutes acting like royalty. Acting through life." He gritted his teeth, saliva and rage coating the inside of his mouth sour, and he spat at her feet.

She grinned smugly, and his hand balled into a fist, the image of throttling her skinny little neck almost arousing. He could jump her, take her down, no matter what training she had as a yakuza wife.

His legs tensed, and she aimed the gun, "Don't," she said simply, tone tranquil. Like blowing a hole in his gut would be merely an inconvenience. She examined Aino, clearly pleased the girl was knocked out.

"So, you just... killed your husband?"

Mimiko smiled, wide and dazzling, her true beauty reserved for only those who could pay or those about to die. She walked backwards to the front door, the gun still aimed at his stomach.

"Of course not. So cliché to kill your own husband. At least, I think so."

Her free hand reached for the door handle, pulling it open to the inky exterior, the green aurora framing a silhouetted figure at the bottom of the steps. The shadow slowly walked up the porch stairs, directly in line with Rocky. Bathed in white and shadows, it stepped forward into the firelight.

Regina.

"Goddammit," he cursed and he felt like he had been stabbed multiple times in the back. She strode in like she walked a runway, right through the front door with her hunting bow and arrow quiver on her shoulder, and a new katana hugging her hip. She briefly scanned Mimiko before turning back to him.

Rocky exhaled a bridled growl of frustration, meeting her wraith-stare above a face covered in a white mask to shield the cold, only her burning blue eyes visible. "You know I had an idea when that bastard Kurt was pulled inside. But how did you bring the bow...?" He leaned his head back against the chair, his foolishness now clear. "The skis, you brought that shit in the ski bag."

The door shut and Regina yanked down the white face and neck gaiter covering her nose and mouth. She'd dressed head to toe in another white snow outfit, perfect for camouflage and bound tight for running. He could sense the adrenaline running through her body; she electrified the entire room with her presence. Her chest heaved as if she had just finished a sprint.

Rocky's calves tensed, his body, readying. But Mimiko lifted the gun at his face, and he stayed put.

"Regina..." he warned. He drew his voice low, the timbre of a dom, and sent her a filthy stare, which she met with equal ire. She was pissed. Fire burned in that stare, and he wondered how she had hidden it for so long. Regina had always been sassy and arrogant with her refined schooling, but she was never a brawler. She was a primped school girl turned high-society with her expensive bags and outfits drying up his checking accounts just like their oil wells.

"Shouldn't have killed Big Daddy, Sugar," she said, slightly breathless and terribly irate.

His jaw fell open in shock.

Mimiko reached for Regina's hip and unclipped the katana—a short, narrow instrument he likened to a slender machete in a scabbard. She extracted it in a fluid motion with one hand and the scabbard flew to the corner of the room, hitting Kurt Muller's corpse. Rocky stared at the dead hitman.

His death was no coincidence. He knew that as soon as he saw the man.

"How did you find out?"

Regina laughed, a false sound, the movement not even reaching her cheeks. "How did I discover you hired that hitman on Big Daddy?"

Her boots, the type she could run or hike a hundred miles in, were caked in snow that shook off as she walked to him. She slowly pulled an arrow from her quiver and held the tip beneath his chin, poking up. He hissed air through his clenched jaw.

"Don't use your fucking AMEX to pay for murder darling. Comes up years later on audits. I'm sure it gave good airline miles, but that's gotta be a lesson in Felony 101. Dumb as a box of rocks, *Rock-ee*."

She twisted the arrow point and it pierced his skin, his nostrils flaring with deep breaths.

"But don't worry, baby, you're not the only dummy." This time her giggle was genuine. "Lord, you should have seen it! Babe, I shoulda joined an improv or some shit. Been an actress! Doing half of this on the fly, luckily all you men are predictable. Forget your little question book, go get it! Wanna investigate a strange light? Hell yeah! Oops, gotta go start up those cars! And the weasel spines on you fellas! Shit, a bucket of reindeer blood and guts hastily thrown and cut and no one even fucking *tried* to examine the wound. See if I was still alive. I nearly cried laughing, sugar."

She pushed the arrow up further, forcing his head upward. He stared at the ceiling's bare logs, his throat exposed. For the first time that night, Rocky was afraid. When he first saw Tetsuya dead, he was anxious at the thought of being caught in the crosshairs. And when he heard his wife was dead, he wasn't worried for his safety, but rather about incarceration. It wouldn't take much investigation to understand Regina's money was nearly gone. She'd played a game and set him up to fall. And when he saw the tires cut, his own plan to leave the others and screech off into the night ruined, the jitters had started in his stomach. But now...

"Black." He swallowed, and the sharp tip of her arrow trailed down, caressing delicate skin over his Adam's apple. Regina stayed silent, so he said it louder. "Black, Regina."

Regina quickly threw off her gloves to grip his scalp, and her French-tipped manicure scraped his skin to pull it down. "Submittin'? You think I'm fucking playing a game, darlin'?" She pushed the arrow up and kept his head still. He flinched, and a warm trickle of blood ran down his neck. Her mouth neared his ear, so close he could hear the tremble in her voice. A quiver that made his muscles involuntarily shiver. A loathing buried for years, crackling her voice like a live wire.

"*I hate what you've all done to me.*"

She straightened again, and the tremble evaporated for a no-foolin' tone. "I slit that dopey-asshole Mattias's throat for making off with a chunk of my inheritance on a deal ruined by his own screwed-up father. Enough money that Big Daddy decided a man, you, should fill that big ole hole he made in my account."

Her claws directed his stare to Kurt Muller's body. "I hired *that* sneaky asshole to come all the way up here to kill another asshole and then shot him through the goddamn throat because he fooled us all into thinking Daddy had a heart attack. I mourned for *months*. Men, men, men. And *you* think I'm playing another dick and dom game? Think a safe word is gonna keep you *safe?*" She crowed with laughter, her energy, her electricity, on a roll, and released him only to swing her fist at his jaw. It connected with more force than he thought possible, more strength that he thought she had, and his neck cricked to the side.

"No, nonono, I'm sorry darlin'. I had dreams that every man, every single goddamn Y chromosome here, ruined in some way. Whether taking, losing, or stealing from me. Last straw for you was when you wouldn't even let me see the one person who made me happy anymore. You don't play by the rules so I tossed out the whole playbook, sugar."

Mimiko stepped behind her, staring Rocky down with those hateful slender eyes, and laid the flat of her blade on his shoulder as if she would just slice across and cut off his head. His hand massaged his jaw, pain radiating along his nerves. Regina's steely gaze left him to look over her shoulder to Mimiko with a softer expression, and the Japanese woman stepped in. They kissed passionately, the katana pressing down beside his neck to show they hadn't forgotten him. Their mouths locked together like puzzle pieces, tongues flashing, breathing into one another familiarly.

When they finally broke apart, fury strained through his forearms clenching his chair. This night wasn't their first encounter; clearly Regina had been unfaithful for some time. He snorted air like a bull, their plan becoming crystal. Regina's high school skills of pickpocketing keys and wallets. The sword and tires. Regina sprinting like a jackrabbit everywhere, doing everything. Her Queen on a chessboard, taking out every little piece. Years of deceit.

"I'm guessing Tetsuya wouldn't enjoy having a cheating dyke for a wife?"

Mimiko, quiet and reserved, held Regina's stare but spoke to him. "He was weak and stupid. Did too many stupid things. Lost that finger because he failed to kill a man, just a common, simple man, but he couldn't do it. Lost us so much money and respect for such a simple, stupid man. Because that's all he was. Simple. I couldn't even fathom having his child, he was so witless. And yes, my *leash* was getting shorter, suffocating." She held her sword knowingly and with practice, looking at it with admiration. "Yakuza have many benefits, but they don't like ex-wives. Dead wives, always. Ex-wives, never."

Regina finally looked away from her lover and leaned close to whisper saccharinely: "Honeybunch, I want you to know you're the biggest piece of shit I've ever met. A real raised-in-a-barn asshole. You did some things right. The shooting range was a smart investment. Been using that well, obviously. But you got too big for your britches off of my fortune. And when the police question me about why you, quite naturally, committed such heinous murders after finding out your wife was unfaithful, I'm not even going to act surprised."

She unslung her bow, and the arrow in her hand rose to nock in. Mimiko stepped away, the sword pointed at him. Rocky's breathing quickened, nearly hyperventilating. "Reg..." he pleaded.

"Naw babe, it's the 21st century. Women like freedom. And I probably would've done it sooner or later, but you just never kill a girl's daddy."

She stepped away and drew the arrow with a strong arm, a mere foot from his face. It quivered with tension, her forearm straining to hold it back.

CARLY

The frantic bull toppled, the arrow in Carly's shoulder and his neck dragging her over the railing with him in a blink. They fell, and time stopped. The air packed her ears like snow until everything was silent. Carly was weightless, tugged only by the anguish in her shoulder. Tugged to the Earth. In the green gloam, for an instant, the majestic reindeer flew.

The bull's head hit the ice and time frantically sped as Carly fell onto its warm body a moment before the sheet cracked. It was a terrible sound she'd never thought she'd hear–a surreal, awful noise. Any rational thoughts were smacked away as both slid into the polar water and an angry current snatched them under.

Carly involuntarily gasped, the shock of the numbing water on her bare neck, her face, her scalp, the hems of her boots and jackets, the bare skin of her tummy. Water filled everywhere, so cold it burned. She was conscious of the traversing space, the water taking them away as it clawed inside everything, clinging like a blanket of frost. Her muscles spasmed from cold shock, her fingers involuntarily squeezing the knife tighter. The knife.

She held a knife.

They bobbed to the surface, the reindeer kicking and thrashing uselessly against the splashing and turbulent water. The current was too fast for its hooves to gain purchase on the river bed. It brayed and snorted, the distressing cries a cacophony above the noisy water and cracking ice that broke and pierced the other side of his body shielding Carly. With choked breath, Carly tugged at the arrowhead in its neck, but it was lodged too deep and he thrashed too much. Every time he jerked, numbing water sucked her down, and a bomb exploded in her shoulder, the shaft moving back and forth through her flesh. This reindeer would kill her soon.

Carried down the fast river, bobbing up and down, she lifted the knife between gasps. Her muscles convulsed of their own accord, fighting the glacial runoff; her body would rebel soon and absolutely ignore her brain. Carly swung and drove the knife up the back of his head, as hard as possible, with all the remaining strength in her sapped body. With all the will left in her freezer-burned soul.

The blade scraped the underside of its skull. Carly assumed she cut the brain because the reindeer stopped thrashing. The current jostled its body, a floating mass of wet fur and dead muscle. Carly clung to him, pushing the corpse forward and onto its side until she rode it like a boogie board. She blinked water away and squinted down the black river they traveled.

Instead of the expected alley of trees, an open expanse of dull white quickly approached. The frozen lake. They had traveled a kilometer in less than a minute. Once they drifted into that lake, she would be sucked under the thick ice, and then Carly would be dead. The end. Even now, her muscles were nearly spent. Buried in cold water and swathed in freezing clothes, her death shroud, Carly neared her finale at breakneck speed.

She craned up, grabbed the arrow shaft, and pulled, the metal slowly slipping out of the reindeer's flesh. It popped out and Carly nearly toppled into the water from the sudden freedom.

Hurryhurryhurry, her mind thought, her lips quivering too much to utter comforting words. Sharp, jagged ice bordered the black water, a barrier to the land. Thick, piercing edges struck the reindeer's body in her stead and flowed by fast. She sucked in stinging air, readying herself, gathering courage, and with gargantuan effort pushed away from its body towards the river's edge.

Her gloved hands scrambled over ice and her heavy legs kicked. Her feet felt like stones with the wet boots, and her stomach strained flat so her body floated behind her. Ice broke beneath her weight, resisting her escape. Carly kicked, pushed, and grabbed more ice until it became thick enough to hold. Her numb feet suddenly pushed against river rock, and her body flailed up like a stiff fish, scrambling in an awkward, painful army crawl, an arrow still in her shoulder, until there was solid ground beneath her body and she kneeled on the snow.

Everything was numb yet everything hurt. Hard to breathe, each breath was so cold, so malevolent, fire ravaged her throat, her nostrils searing. Carly grew up in the desert yet she was burning in this desolate frozen land. She had only been in the water for two minutes, less. But she was dying now. She would soon be dead. All she wanted was to lay on the snow.

Ignoring the desire, she looked to the arrow in her shoulder and, through her waning strength and groggy mind, was surprised. The arrow that killed Kurt was wooden, sturdy, and old. This was metallic, the black shaft cold and shiny, and explained why it hadn't broken in the fall. The metal head, washed of blood, glistened silver, and Carly twisted until it unscrewed. She could have laughed or cried or howled in agony as the arrowhead dismantled in less than ten seconds and the dull end remained.

She peeked at the exit wound through the rip it had made. Little blood. No arteries. She couldn't leave it in; every time she moved, the shaft lanced tendrils of hot electricity in her shoulder, the water dangerously numbing the pain. Pain was good. Pain meant she was still alive. Her nerves were still working to tell her she had a fucking arrow in her shoulder. In one swift motion, her opposite hand reached back, meeting the fletching at the arrow's tail. She yanked it fast, too fast for her brain to understand what she was doing as it ripped out of her body.

Carly fell to the ground. Snow scratched her face and she rolled onto her back. Breathing was problematic, the air too cold for her frozen lungs. Nothing was getting in and her face had turned numb long ago. Was her mouth still open? The convulsions of her limbs were lessening, and though Carly wasn't trained for the cold, she knew that was bad. Convulsions meant your body still had a chance.

The sky unexpectedly erupted in green fire, a resurgence of Foxfire, kerosene on a flame, the brightest Carly had seen yet. Enough to illuminate the ground around her and the river at her feet. Despite all her pain, she was transfixed and wondered if she had actually died and this was heaven's doorway, another quack legend. Her quivering hand reached skyward just as a smear of red flowed through the neon green, like blood running down a grassy field. Carly pushed her heavy body up onto her elbows, simply staring at the phenomena as she froze.

Ice cracked in the river she'd just escaped, small but constant breaks, and she squinted. A body floated atop the current, occasionally caught by a sharp edge, as if the ice wanted to catch it. It bobbled by, and Carly recognized Mattias's happy, round face, now slack and watching the aurora above him.

Drawing on her reserves of strength, Carly stood, intending to call to him. But his face was too relaxed, his body limp in the water. He was already dead and if she tried to catch him, she would be dead too. She recalled their last words: save the daughter.

He floated towards the river's exit, a white shelf of ice, and then he was gone. A sacrifice pulled beneath. Carly imagined him under the lake's glacial surface, the world upside down, watching the hazy green aurora with its own streak of blood as if staring through a bathroom's frosted glass. An icy tomb.

Movemovemove, Carly's mind pleaded, less quick, less sharp this time. Move where? Back to the lodge? Back to the bridge? Back to the igloos with their see-through walls? Nowhere felt safe. But the wet clothes couldn't stay on her body. If the water hadn't killed her, wet clothes would. Already she felt akin to the permafrost trees and their frozen outsides. With stiff movements, she began removing her jacket, but a howl stopped her hand.

It was the uncanny human cry of an escaped husky. Close. Maybe a stone's throw. At first, it was a lone howl, sad and unearthly against the hoary night. Then the one was joined by two, three, ten. A chorus of howls erupted along the lake's abyssal-black shoreline. The deeper howls of wolves, the growl of far-off bears, a screech of hunting owls, the yowls of hungry predators.

The aurora suddenly flushed neon red in a spectacular burst. Lava in the sky burned the green away, and Carly had to shield her eyes or go blind. When she opened them, the fire was gone, the verdant green resuming its gentle, slender ribbons. The howls also ceased, and the surreal quiet of padded snow between furred trees resumed.

She held her breath. The numbing of her muscles and body was forgotten. The forest and snow held a new tension. It felt like it was readying for explosion it couldn't escape, and Carly heard something she didn't understand.

A crack split the winter night.

It was like ancient stones grinding and sliding. Or muted lightning stabbing the earth. Carly never experienced anything as alien as that sound and her cold heart beat faster. Her gaze drew to the far middle of the lake. Solid ice calved, breaking apart in great spurts, like a glacier splitting and tumbling over and over. Displaced water splashed between the cracks. Carly squinted as white ice lifted, something rising through the center, no more than a hundred meters away.

A nebulous creature, black as tar, burst through the sheet, clawing out of the water, nails scratching the ice, and an earth-shuddering, clotted growl reverberated through the air. It rumbled through the forest, and Carly flinched when the forest responded in welcome. The trees shook snow from their branches, sleepy critters chittered, and the air brimmed with frost that touched her eyelashes.

She mindlessly stepped away. That growl. It was cavernous. Endless. Timeless. Hungry. Mean. The shape pulled itself up from the ice hole and stood on all fours, and Carly stumbled, aghast at its size. It dwarfed the trees on the far shore. She scrambled backward and her heart began racing when it growled, reminiscent of distant thunder. Followed by the thud of hooves.

Carly ran.

Her boots were heavy, her body heavier and dragged down by wet, frosty clothes layered in thin ice. But she ran. Her shoulder was numb, probably bleeding, leaking her life blood and any warmth.

But she ran.

Ran along the river's edge; ran from growling and the thud of hooves on snow chasing her at a distance; ran though the vibrations of its heavy body shaking the earth; ran, flinching as trees crunched from a massive weight nudging them aside; ran until her breath was hot and harried and a little bit of life returned to her nearly hypothermic body; ran until the bridge was above, and she scrambled up the small hill and returned onto the driveway; ran across clear, packed snow, hearing growls shimmy the very air she huffed in and out; ran all the way to the lit lodge, warm and inviting, though it would not deter the monster chasing her. Carly ran up the stairs and burst through the door, the warm interior sizzling her skin.

Her knees collapsed to the floor and the door mercifully swung shut.

Three figures stared, bug-eyed, at her entrance, and Carly wasn't even concerned by the once-dead Regina pulling a vicious looking bow on her husband. She gasped through burning breaths, enough to warn them.

"Run."

REGINA

"... I'm not even going to act surprised," she said with so much satisfaction it almost sounded like Regina was just joking around. No, when the police questioned her, Regina would give perfunctory tears and sniffles–there were so many dead, so of course–but in no way would she act surprised. Rocky was a grade-A asshole, abuser, and murderer. She had just gotten to him first, as every fed-up and abused wife should.

She nocked the arrow, her breath shaky. Jesus, she felt so elated, every molecule in her body wanted to orgasm, wanted to revel in all she worked hard to accomplish with destiny's help. Everything, the well-timed reindeer carcass and blood, her memory of the trails, the distracting aurora, Tetsua's timely exit–it was all a miraculous serendipity, a convergence of fate, leading to this moment she dreamed of for six years. Maybe at first she hadn't dreamed of murdering him, spending months gathering them all in one isolated place to murder all the fucking birds with all the sharp stones in her pocket. But still, she certainly dreamed of watching Rocky lose blood the way he made her bleed dignity.

She pulled the string taut. Maybe it started the first time he ordered her dinner for her. Or the first time he had ignored her for her daddy. Or when he celebrated Big Daddy accepting his proposal. Or maybe when he casually raped his wife, easy to do and forget in Texas. Likely when he hid her passport so she couldn't use her money and take a trip to Japan 'needlessly' to see her friend. Certainly when she came across the assassin's paper trail. Definitely when foolish Mattias started advertising his poor investment world-wide after a decade of silence.

She drew further, tension shaking the arrowhead, and his nostrils flared. Sweat and fear gloriously creased his brow like a slimy bullfrog. He was scared. Terrified. Regina had never been scared of Rocky, but shit, she'd been angry...

"Reg..." he whined, and it was nails on a chalkboard to her ears.

Men, men, men, perpetrators of their own demise. Rocky, Tetsuya, Kurt, Mattias. They had all fucked over the wrong Texan.

"Naw babe, it's the 21st century. Women like freedom. And I probably would've done it sooner or later but you just never kill a girl's daddy." Her heartbeat thumped in her ears, a racing mustang with hooves too fast, too excited to care for anything other than releasing that arrow. But she'd worked too long to squander this pleasure.

Her finger nearly released when the door burst open and a frosted, shivering figure fell inside. Wind followed her in and the fire squealed as it fled up the chimney. The door swung closed and there were three full seconds of silence in the room before the figure gasped.

"Run."

Regina blinked, shocked, her gaze flicking between her husband and the dead woman with frozen hair, gasping for breath.

Mimiko hissed in Japanese. "You didn't kill her?!"

The bow's string fractionally relaxed, Rocky's hands flexing into balls as they were want to do, eager for a fight, his bravado returning. Regina retreated, putting space between them. "I nailed her to a fucking reindeer and she was drowned in the frozen river. She should be dead." She glanced away from her husband to disheveled Carly. "Hell, she's nearly there."

Mimiko raised the katana with a strong, rigid arm, staring down the cool steel and about to cut off Carly's head, when the half-frozen woman began undressing quickly. Her jacket and pants were crisp with frost, and she moved fast and sure. Regina's feet readjusted defensively like she was an opposing magnet, unsure of this ploy or trick. Mimiko frowned, also puzzled at this strange turn of events.

Several things then happened all at once. A jarring, guttural howl resonated outside, maybe far in the distance, but whatever made it was undeniably large. The sound, thrumming the very walls of the log cabin, startled Aino awake, and she jolted upright as if electrocuted. Carly scrambled on hands and knees, naked, and over to the fire and chair opposite Rocky to a set of outdoor clothes, laying as if waiting for her.

The lovers started at the growl, Regina's arrow lowering while Mimiko raised her sword to the doorway as if a different type of visitor would burst through next.

"What the fuck was that?" Rocky exclaimed, bolting to stand and gripping the back of the chair. Everyone now ignored Carly, stepping into the clothes and shivering, steam rising from her wet, naked skin in the fire's heat. The growl tapered, a vacuum of sound in its stead, until the cries of the huskies Regina released earlier broke the silence.

The unsettling howls continued, eerie singing to accompany the unnerving setting, and everyone slowly turned to Carly, pulling pants over white and shaking legs. The wound in her shoulder was pink and puckered but clean, a sliver of exposed flesh from the open X-shaped wound.

"Hey! What the fuck was that!?" Regina demanded, mirroring her husband—except where he was scared, she was angry. Wrathful even, as if Carly had brought an unwanted guest to an exclusive party. A shirt went over the Australian's head; she seemed unconcerned with the others in the room, behaving like she didn't give a rat's ass for the machinations of the two armed women.

Carly zipped up the jacket. Her wild eyes, framed by icy brows now melting, searched the room and landed on groggy Aino on the floor. She spoke without addressing anyone in particular. "Big, that's what it is." She slipped on her wet boots and pulled the beanie over her stiff hair.

"We have to go, kid," she said through lips still pale with near frostbite and crossed the space, a battlefield only a moment ago, her hand reaching for Aino. The girl took it and stood, wobbling. Aino did not reply, blinking several times, clearing her head, and hobbled to the front door.

Mimiko, small but formidable, stepped in front of the pair, and Regina remembered Rocky. Standing idly, he was waiting for someone to tell him what to do. She once again pulled her arrow at him.

Mimiko held the katana directly before Carly's face. "No one leaves," she simply stated with Japanese efficiency.

The unknown beast thundered again, joining the caterwaul of the much smaller huskies. Mimiko's left eye twitched, breaking the facade of her reserved demeanor, and her grip on the sword tightened. She glanced quickly to Regina for assurance, or perhaps permission to stab the Australian in the face, when the growl rumbled again. *Much* closer, this time.

Carly's hand brushed the sword aside effortlessly. "Feel free to stay." She sidestepped Mimiko and picked up another hat from the door, dressing Aino. "Kid, do you know a trail that can get us out of here?"

The howls grew tumultuous, closer to the house, perhaps beginning to surround it. Aino stuttered, "Out..outside? Shouldn't we... stay inside?"

Carly tugged the hat down Aino's forehead and her voice trembled with cold. "Inside is not going to stop that thing. Do you know of any trails? Something tight? Trees close together?"

Regina walked warily, circling her hostages, not sure they were anymore, and listened to Aino and the wail of animals in the breeze. The woman was serious; she wanted to run from the howls. This wasn't some ploy, talking her way out of being collateral damage in a vengeful spree.

Aino squeezed her eyes shut, blocking out the clamor, and she nodded her head. "Yes, yes, there is an old track behind the barn."

Carly reached for the door, but Regina stepped between her and it. Mimiko raised her katana to keep Rocky from doing anything stupid. The bow and arrow were still in Regina's hands but she had lost the inclination to use them, her intrigue winning out. "What is it then?"

Carly exhaled, trembling with deathly cold, or fear, or maybe both. "I don't know. It's...big...and runs on all fours, maybe." Her hand weaved around a confused Regina for the doorknob.

"A bear?"

She pulled open the door, the choir of dogs meeting them, and Regina let her, the new mystery too puzzling. Mimiko and a cautious Rocky followed, their feud and his imminent death postponed. Carly spoke over her shoulder. "If it is, it's no bear I know."

She ran with Aino along the porch, avoiding the front steps. Regina also stepped outside, cautiously, her bow and arrow nocked. She kept the two women in her peripheral should she suddenly need to shoot Carly in the back. Again. The bitter chill burned her bare cheeks and she scanned the treeline. The blood-curdling growl of a predator emanated to the left and from the bend of the driveway, nearing the lodge. Regina frowned.

As they left the steps, they saw the aurora had dimmed, weak streams of light pulsing as dying embers. Regina walked confidently into the clear space as Mimiko and Rocky remained on the porch.

"Hell, can't be bigger than that buffalo I killed and quartered," she muttered and readied her shooting stance. She drew up her neck scarf, covering her mouth that hid her breath, and pulled the arrow back, its cool shaft against her cheek, the string tight.

Rattling, horrid breath and the *crunchcrunchcrunch* of footsteps on snowpack grew louder as it came closer. A black silhouette moved, but not where Regina was looking—not where you would expect a lumbering oaf of a bear to walk. It was nearly fifteen feet higher than she anticipated as it rounded the tree line.

Mimiko gasped.

"What the summabitch...?" Rocky added.

Regina's pulse, steady all night as she ran between the woods, sprinting to catch everyone coming out of that house, anticipating what they would need, what they would do, three steps before they did, began beating like a stampede lived in her chest. A war drum signaling the end.

The goliath stepped slowly, snorting, sniffing the ground, and in the dim light, darker shadows against shadows revealed the face of a bear and a head crowned in brambles of white bone—odd, jagged angles reaching heavenward. It turned to Regina with infernal light in two eyes. Two jade stones on fire.

It was the Devil.

Regina's tremulous fingers released the arrow, sensing rather than seeing her aim was true, hitting it right between those fiery, feral eyes.

It should have buried through its bone but instead, the beast snuffled like a bee stung its face. Its irritation flamed to madness, its huffs growing faster and hotter; rank breath billowed like steam, and a great cloven hoof stepped out of the mass of hair and flesh.

A rigid step.

Another.

More.

Regina's hand darted behind her head, plucking another arrow, notching, pressing it against her cheek for a blink before she fired.

The beast cantered, and a terrifying hammer Regina felt in her bones shook the ground. The dark limbs and muscles warmed up, growing faster and angrier.

Another arrow fired, fletching whipped Regina's hair, scoring through the air, the distance closing.

Fast.

Bigger than any buffalo, it was a loaded train with a raging engine. A mass of fur and horn and muscle and hoof and other body parts that shouldn't belong to only one creature, swathed in a black fur that sucked light, a black void, an inky reaper, all pummeled towards Regina, and her tiny arrows shot at its head, its chest, its heart.

It was unstoppable.

Regina glanced over her left shoulder to the porch. Rocky was long gone, and Mimiko stood alone. Small but strong, her katana was aloft, and her disbelief showed on her face. Regina reached for her last arrow, pulling it even as they shared a knowing glance, and fired the remaining ten feet into the great portal of its opening mouth, lined with crude, jagged bone.

The arrow pierced something important inside and it abruptly pulled short.

Glory, victory, domination over killing something bigger than herself, taking something special and claiming it, flowed through Regina with relief. The creature reared on massive haunches as if to fall and instead tipped forward to its hooves, the colossal head and maw opening as if it would detach.

Regina wasn't fast enough. Who could dodge lightning? she thought for the last time as the jaw enveloped her head and down her collarbone, teeth punching her breast bone and back like railroad nails. She smelled pine, the last of her senses before it bit hard and ripped her head away from her body.

MIMIKO

Mimiko blinked at the scene in the driveway and the frost lacing her eyelashes was abruptly gone, and a flower petal brushed her cheek. Dancing across her skin in the warm air. Sakura fell from the blue sky like a sheet of light rain, a cascade of heavenly delight. Only for one day. Mimiko's teenage and willowy hand reached beyond the protection of her wagasa for several dark pink petals to fall on her hand and sleeve of her kimono. She raised them to her eye level, the white Nijo Castle looming in the background. Delicate and as small as silk strands, she blew on the petals and they resumed their journey to the ground.

"Mimi, Mimi…" Himari, her kami-san hissed from her spot on the ground.

Mimiko refrained from rolling her eyes and turned to her employer on the picnic blanket. Another Maiko, one of her house-sisters and another Geisha in training, sat at the far end with an older gentleman, and she gently giggled at something inane. Gentle laughter—the business man's confidence booster. Himari gestured for Mimiko to lean down to her and she complied, bending her pressed knees to the side instead of her stiff waistline.

"Why don't you take a walk?" she said innocently, the hissing hag gone.

Mimiko understood and nodded, turning to the castle grounds and the many cherry blossoms fully bloomed and now falling. Tourists and locals littered the space between trees, hanami well underway with drinking and merriment. Young girls her own age and dressed in more comfortable clothes snapped pictures with one another to commemorate the special time of the year.

Mimiko weaved through the trees, through the crowd, parting for her with her little umbrella and the shuffle of her traditional shoes, her legs restricted by the cumbersome kimono, all designed so she appeared more demure. Feebler than what she really was. Escape was slow and nearly impossible. Many people stared at her painted face and groomed hair, tinkling with trinkets. Some tourists bravely asked for pictures she would acquiesce to with few words, no smile, and an erect spine. Playing her role. Others who approached were men, speculating how much it would cost them to spend the day with her. Cowards who wouldn't even ask but were happy to observe one of Kyoto's rare species like an animal in a zoo.

Eventually, Mimiko's mind wandered to other things rather than finding herself a patron for the day, wondering how many more days she would need one, every day spent searching until someone was suitable, rich enough, to take her out of it. Every day wondering if her mother still lived on the streets up in Osaka. She walked through the raining petals, heading towards the castle's ground, aware of their annual demonstration of medieval Japan. Men on horses and old samurai clanged swords and shouted in deep timbres, as an eager crowd surrounded and hid them.

A giggle, harsh but not unpleasant, interrupted her mind's wandering, and Mimiko spied the source. A white woman, a girl, with long blonde locks curled tight stood beneath a tree. She dressed as a harajuku girl, bright colors and short skirts over unicorn tights with platform shoes. Mimiko stopped to watch the scene, her eyes glued to the girl. She had...something. Charisma, a natural attraction drawing everyone's gaze. A group of salarymen, cheeks flushed red from too many chu-his, stood around her. A hand touched her shoulder, another hand on her hip, fingers making peace signs, too many hands hidden and likely wandering and touching places they shouldn't. But then a white and lithe hand made a quick movement, a blink and you miss it moment. The girl's hand slid around the back of a man, and into his side pocket, a small wallet escaping, and then the hand was gone.

The group took another picture from another phone, and the girl grinned wider. It was the most exciting, thrilling thing Mimiko ever saw.

The men left her, happy and slapping each other playfully, no one protesting or looking around on the ground for missing property. The Gaijin harajuku moved through the grounds and Mimiko trailed casually behind at a distance, eager for more. The girl was stopped several more times as she made her way through the orchard, halting twice more for photos and stealing wallets. Mimiko, forgetting herself and her role, laughed aloud from her place in the distance when the second drunk and handsy man had his wallet skillfully stolen.

Eventually the girl reached the end of the cherry trees, the gravel lot for entry to the castle's inner walls and Mimiko lost sight of her in a wave of people following a tour guide's red flag. Mimiko had ignored the pointed stares of the crowd, avoiding those intent on a picture with her, instead following this girl as if she was gravity and Mimiko a helpless satellite. But when she also reached the gravel, the girl was gone.

"Finally coming to say hello?"

Mimiko spun, surprised, and the girl was at her shoulder with a mischievous smile. Her brain scrambled for the correct English. She no longer had English lessons, but all children were taught pleasantries since the first grade. But the girl never gave her a chance to answer as her swift fingers plucked Mimiko's fan from where it was wedged in her obi-belt and flicked it open, holding it to cover every-thing below her eyes.

"Or maybe you want a picture?" she said in Japanese with a lowered, seductive voice a young girl shouldn't have.

Mimiko laughed. "I can't afford it."

The girl lowered the fan, the mischief gone, and instead she smirked and arched her eyebrow. Her gaze moved up and down Mimiko's best traditional kimono, a special occasion for hanami, and then up to her painted face, squinting and leaning forward, as if trying to peer past the white powder to her real face beneath. Her own delicate nose and wide blue eyes were the most fascinating things Mimi had ever seen, not contacts, not surgical or fancy makeup–wide and vibrant and filled with a soul eager to put them to use. She returned the fan back to Mimi's belt, her fingers digging inside and down the belt and then assumed her arm, leading them away from the cherry blossoms, Mimi's open umbrella on their backs.

"Shall we watch the performance?" she casually asked, already walking them across the open space. Mimiko smiled, unsure and bewitched, and allowed herself to be led. Using her free hand, the girl unclipped an extension of her hair and placed it in a bag hanging from her belt, her long locks turned to a straight bob. She pulled a cord around her chest, and the top she wore fell down and over her skirt, a longer skirt of beige now hiding the ostentatious colors and thick shoes. She finally reached into the same bag and pulled a wet wipe, deftly ridding her face of the vibrant makeup and slick contouring of her nose and cheeks. In all but a minute, she had transformed into just another Western tourist traveling Kyoto. A chameleon, hiding in plain sight. Mimiko blinked at her as she threw away the wipe and shook out her hair.

"I'm Regina," she spoke in English, smiling.

"Mimiko," she replied, dumbstruck.

They joined the crowd, two or three rows from the front, watching the 2pm demonstration. A team of reenactors dressed as warriors from feudal Japan set themselves in front of the castle on a large but low stage. A story of some sort was happening, though Mimiko wasn't interested in the slightest. Regina dropped her arm as they watched the narrator holler the story, actors behind him each on their own course from firing long-bows at targets or swordplay in some bid to defeat an oni devil lingering on the edges. Mimiko eyed the girl beside her, slyly. She couldn't be older than her own age of sixteen, but seemed so much...more. Maybe it was the stealing. Stealing seemed like an 'experienced' game. Stealing well needed skill.

They were silent for a time, Mimiko sensing the girl was also only pretending to watch– stealing glances at each other, examining some part of her dress. Their bodies were only inches apart and Mimiko swore she felt heat radiate off her. Tension swelled in the small space between them, Mimiko fidgeting slightly in ways that had been beaten out of her this last year until Regina finally quietly asked,"How much would it cost to... spend the night together?"

Mimiko was taken back, and didn't bother to explain that she wasn't that way...yet. Instead, she countered in a playful banter, "Are you rich?"

Regina paused, her bottom lip hanging open, then frowned. "No, I guess I'm not so rich anymore." She pulled a man's wallet from her small sack. "Wait, maybe I am," she laughed and fingered the 10,000 yen notes. Mimiko looked at it; it was no small amount, a night for karaoke and drinks and expensive taxis late at night. But not enough to get her out of a life of servitude, nor for a night with a real Geisha. She said nothing and Regina dropped the wallet into her sack. Actors with swords had stopped their fight and were now passing through the audience, allowing them to see the genuine weapons, answering questions and spewing random facts. They watched him pass, a handsome young man in his costume.

Regina whispered conspiratorially, "Do you think I'd get away stealing that sword?"

"Do you like swords?"

Regina frowned and her eyes roamed the performance stage again. "No, I think I'd like to try that bow more."

"That's a shame, I would have liked to see you steal a sword. I think I would like a sword in the future."

Regina smiled at her with glinting eyes that moved down to her mouth, only half-painted red until she finished her training. "I think I would like to kiss you in the future," she replied nonchalantly. Mimiko's face grew hot, her mind going blank with no witty repartee. Regina held her gaze with a cautious grin until Mimi decided she would like that too and slowly copied her grin. Beneath the wide and cavernous sleeve, she reached for Regina's fingers, and it felt like thousands of eyes were on her, doing something so forward. Something so frowned upon. Absolutely forbidden. They intertwined fingers, only the tips, in secret, and Mimiko felt something spark inside her that never had before.

The actor in the oni mask, a fiery red demon with horns and snarling teeth, growled at the crowd. A monster growled and she blinked again, frost stiffening her eyelids.

The monster, the kaiju, death masquerading as a beast, lumbered around the snowy bend and Mimiko was awestruck. She had adlibbed about bone and crown earlier, quick thinking and a diversion for their improvised machinations, all inspired by the large painting that hung above the fireplace. But this was her lies brought to life and turned against her. Unlike anything she had ever seen or imagined, there was nothing like it in this world, and that's how she knew it was from another.

Rocky, Regina's vile jailer, mumbled incoherently behind her shoulder and his loafish lumber ran down the porch. Mimiko was too distracted as he followed the women already past the barngarage where Regina had slashed the car's tires earlier.

Mimiko was about to instruct Regina–headstrong woman who considered herself indestructible–to return so they could barricade themselves inside. But Regina had already drawn her bow and fired without hesitation. In a flutter of Mimiko's eyelashes, the monster charged Regina. Thirty meters turned to twenty turned to five and her last arrow finally made the brute rear and then stomp vengefully forward.

Regina's body was engulfed far down its gullet. Before the vomit reached Mimiko's esophagus, its jaws had already bitten her clavicle. Teeth crunched, breaking bone, and the sight of Regina's legs raising off the ground and seizing in a million tiny little jerks, made Mimiko wretch. Her eyes squeezed shut as pudding and reindeer meat splattered the porch. The sounds, the gnawing bone grinding bone, of wet crunches and gurgles and blood spilling to sloppy ice-snow and huffing, dirty breaths invaded Mimiko's ears, and she squeezed her eyes harder as if that would stop them.

When there was nothing left to expel, she opened her watery and sore eyes. Regina's body, the head and collarbone gone, lay on its side, spilling life like a weak hose; and the monster, with the vague shape of a vast, antlered bear, quietly crunched a muscle-strewn bone.

Regina's hand still clenched her bow, fingers spasming around the handle.

Mimiko was cold. Freezing. The purge lacing her mouth stiffened in the air. But a new heat smoldered in her belly, more saliva pooling her cheeks in anticipation of an eruption. A portent of internal rage, turmoil, blind fury. Bridled wrath vibrated deep within her body, Tetsuya's katana shook in her clutch and its keen point scraped the porch's wood.

A lock of Regina's honey-platinum hair fell from between its teeth, viscid with saliva.

Mimiko's molars ground, ire strained her entire face, quaking her whole being.

The creature's head tilted to the umbral sky, and the lock of lovely hair slowly receded into the open jaws. Regina's head was swallowed.

Mimiko brought the katana across her forehead in *ko gasumi*, steadying her balance. Forgetting any other training, she raised it behind her head, point out, and screamed. All her pain and rage released in one cathartic shriek. Tears and vomit dripped down her chin, and she sprinted the distance across the porch, leaping from the top stair and swinging down behind the villain's neck.

The blade plunged deep inside its body, like cutting foggy air. Like there was nothing, but it stopped all the same, and her fists clenching the braided handle brushed against birch and moss carpet. For a fraction of a second, an eternity, Mimiko hung off the katana, a meter off the ground, and yanked it down with her whole weight, trying for more flesh if any lay behind the hair of branches and moss.

Teeth tenderly wrapped around her shoulder, and then bit, piercing through cloth and skin like butter, excruciating agony blinding her senses from anything else. Mimiko howled, the fangs separating her sinew from her bones, torrid breath blowing across her distorted features. She couldn't stop crying or screaming. She didn't want to. She wouldn't know how. Her grip on the katana released; gravity pulled her weight down against the teeth, and a limb parted from her body.

Mimiko fell to the snow. The naked skin of her upper arm hung from the creature's jaw, and her koi fish tattoo swam in blood and saliva. Her howls rent the air between gasps, and the snow beneath her face began melting, warmth spreading everywhere. Hot coppery liquid warmed her mouth and cheek. Her sight shook with bodily convulsions, and the green sky dimmed. The beast shook his head with her limb in his mouth and blood speckled across their bodies like soft rain. It padded away from her spot on the ground and toward the forest. Soft rain. Soft snow. Sakura falling. Mimiko reached with her remaining hand across the pool of melted blood-snow to Regina's limp one and intertwined their fingertips.

AINO

Carly's gloved hand weakly gripped Aino's arm, dragging her down the porch. Her head throbbed, but cold air was a salve for muddy minds, and slowly the fuzziness cleared as her body set to motion, blood pumping and moving. They reached the porch's end and stepped off without hesitation.

"Wasn't that... wasn't the American woman dead?" she asked, glancing at the three others stepping onto the porch. The dead woman was quite clearly alive and her inner organs still intact. Aino and Carly were in the trees and the house hidden from sight.

"Yeah, I don't know, kid. She's the last thing I'm worried about. Where's the trail?"

Aino's sight adjusted to the undergrowth's gloom, her head still confused. She planted her feet obstinately on the ground and forced Carly to stop. Closing her eyes, she recalled the many paths of her grandfather. A labyrinth within the trees.

A roar shuddered the forest, echoing through the dense bodies of flora and into Aino's chest like she was standing too close to the stage at a concert. Something tried to pull her back, her heart on a

142

string, tugging her back to the house. Her eyes opened and she pointed confidently.

"Aim left, a wider trail will soon open."

Carly's whole body quivered when she nodded, but she moved forward anyway, if not a fraction slower than when they started. Aino bounced ahead of her, hopeful muscle memory would return to the ways she often walked as a child. The warmth of the cabin slowly evaporated as the deep winter night brushed her face, the tip of her nose numbing. Aino glanced overhead as they walked with the wind pushing against their faces. Revontulet burned the sky, and Aino couldn't remember ever seeing it so bright for so long. An unearthly green silhouetted the clumpy snow-laden branches of the close pines and spruces. Waves within waves, oceans among oceans.

A bell tinkled ahead—only for a breath. Aino stopped in her tracks, silencing the crunch of their feet. Another tinkle rang directly in front of them, and she discerned the start of the trail, really just a depression of the land in a continuous line. Where old feet had tread thousands of times before, pressed and hardened, the forest reshaping itself to her grandfather's will. A titan among the trees. More importantly, she saw the faint outline of the back of a sleigh and beyond that, a reindeer's rump pierced with an arrow.

Aino murmured in wonder. Another howl startled the reindeer and it flinched forward a step, the bell at its neck ringing.

"Well, that's lucky." Carly's voice shivered from the cold, and Aino was distracted from the intimidating growls behind them.

"Are you going to be alright?"

Instead of answering, Carly side stepped around her and to the sleigh, the harnessed reindeer pawed the ground nervously as she approached. Showing him her trembling, raised hands, she slowly moved them to grip the arrow shaft, sunk a solid two inches into the fleshy rump. Carly strained, her other hand on the soft fur to minimize the impact, and the arrow abruptly slid out. The reindeer's flank shivered in a cascade and it skittered forward, the sleigh dragging behind it.

"Can you drive?" Carly asked through pale lips, her voice far too soft, a wraith of her previous self. She reached for the reindeer's harness and threw away the attached bell.

Aino nodded and stopped still at the sound of running. Heavy feet running. The two women swung their heads to the trail behind them, and Aino realized for the first time her hand no longer clenched the rifle. She was naked and vulnerable.

Suddenly, Rocky ran from under a darkened eave of snow, hysteria on his handsome features. Aino steeled herself, her face, her body, should he suddenly use his massive weight against her.

Instead, he blurted, "We gotta go!" To emphasize his statement, a woman's high-pitched shriek, angry and tormented, reverberated through the quiet trees, startling Aino and the reindeer. She nodded in agreement, even as he moved to the sleigh. Three was a lot for one reindeer, too much. But the two women together maybe equaled another man. Had the reindeer been smaller, it might not even be able to move and Aino would need to hop on and off to run with it, pushing from behind.

Carly watched Rocky as he climbed into the sleigh without asking. Aino guessed she was too tired to fight about anything. She needed to save her nearly spent energy for running, staying warm, and staying alive. They shared a cautious stare, but Carly then also sat in the sleigh at his feet. The grizzled roar of the mysterious beast hollered nearby, a deep, glottal cry almost resembling a wolf's call. Calling for others. But for what? Or for who?

The reindeer spooked, and the sleigh started pulling away. Aino jogged to catch up and stepped onto the back footboards, her gloves brushing away layered snow on the handlebar. Her grandfather's mannerisms, his gentle handling of the family reindeer, his insistent *shushshushshush* to urge them forward while little Aino sat as a child in the low sleigh–all returned to her in blink. The decade she had been away and off this land was only a moment.

She mimicked his noises, hoping this reindeer recalled the one who raised him. It jumped in stride, encouraged by her call, or maybe by fear of the grizzled roar. The sleigh traveled down the track, the burdensome weight sliding heavily in the hushed woods. The trail curved, a slight decline providing momentum, all sense of direction lost.

"Where are we going?" Aino called.

The faint breeze now blew at her back, forward over the pair, and she was sure they heard her. In the very front, Carly didn't answer; after a moment of listening to the reindeer's hooves, Rocky turned instead. "Who cares! Just go for as long as the reindeer can and *away.*"

Aino blinked away frost settling on her eyelashes and squinted ahead. The air prickled; it was maybe fifteen or twenty below and her cheeks already stung. But life, energy, began overtaking her fatigue as she leaned the sleigh side to side, deftly guiding it around bends, and old ingrained habits woke.

Where did this trail lead? The reindeer followed a path Aino didn't know in the dark, his trot unfaltering as they weaved between ancient pillars lacquered in glistening ice. Most likely he would circle their land, and if they had turned south from the lodge, they would soon be crossing the family's land boundary. Would there be a fence? Or could they just ride forever? Forever in the dark.

The light wind, really just a breath now, carried a peculiar noise, and Aino tilted her head to hear better. Not the cry of an animal, but a *burrr*, like a house cat purring. A distant memory, only a whisper of deja vu, caressed Aino's brain. Her grandfather, driving the sleigh in the blue twilight, his face lit in happiness, a deep feeling of serenity. Hooves hitting the ground.

The decline of the hill deepened, and Aino's attention was stolen as the weight of the three shifted forward, the reindeer needing to run with the sleigh rather than pull it. As they dashed through the alley of dark trees, Aino was tempted to stomp on the claw brake, slowing their descent should the reindeer falter and hit one of them. But the trees cleared all at once, the packed forest ending, and the reindeer ran down a gentle-sloping open hill facing opposite a similar one—a lovely low valley gleaming bright with unblemished snow. Trees lined the tops of the two tall hills and the reindeer plowed forward, kicking up thick snow. Carly and Rocky were sprayed with the occasional flurry, neither moving, but Aino watched Rocky snuggle into his coat and endure the snow and freezing conditions.

Aino had no recollection of this hill or this part of their land. The reindeer, however, continued unerringly, swerving around little mounds, undoubtedly sizeable rocks beneath the pack, and again Aino credited her grandfather. His little paths wound through the forest like arteries in a body.

Had she heard that expression before? Arteries in a body? Like the forest was alive? Everything connected to nature, to life. He had said so much, so many strange things she and her young, uninterested ears credited as crazy and senile. She had humored him many times and now felt ashamed and saddened she hadn't appreciated his wisdom. Wisdom buried within layers and then lost because the elderly wanted to teach and youth never wanted to listen.

The reindeer neared the bottom of the valley and she *shusshhed* him forward in anticipation, urging him faster so his momentum would volley them up on the waiting hill. He bounded forward, knees kicking high to pull across the bottom and up the other side. The momentum kept for a few seconds, but their weight rolled back, and the reindeer was too young. Aino stepped off the footholds and began to run, all her weight and energy pushing the hand bar, staring down at the trampled snow. Her breath and lungs strained against the biting cold, and she remembered Wilholm's warning. *The cold bites you like teeth!* She ran and that same cold gnawed at her lungs.

CARLY

The sleigh took off, only slow at first, but then Carly felt her weight shift and instinctively knew her burden to the poor reindeer wasn't so great. The beast that had risen from the lake–the one with the roar she would never forget, the one she was sure would replay over and over in her mind for years to come–was behind them, and they were moving. For the first time since finding Tetsuya's frozen body, Carly was optimistic. They were moving. Mattias's round face with his puppy-dog eyes burned her mind. She had saved the bloody daughter.

Carly's body, her core, trembled, and she was reminded of the reindeer's shivering flank. She wanted to laugh at the simple comparison, but instead blew heated air down into her coat, not feeling it in the slightest. She no longer felt the wind on her face, her skin numb. She stared forward at the reindeer's running backside, and then to the forest around them. The trees whizzed by, and then it was Kurt staring at her. Her eyes welled, stinging, and she closed them, only to see more of Kurt's frozen and milky eyes, open above the arrow sticking out of his neck, feathers brushing his chin.

Her quirky new boyfriend. Something stuck in her throat and she could no longer swallow. Kurt had been a strange man. Everything from his casually approaching her with ease and asking her out, his extravagant dates contradictory to his quiet manner, and finished by rough sex he would clean off with hot, scalding showers. He had asked her on this trip and almost seemed anxious she might decline. Carly liked strange and unusual.

But she had found him too late, an old story. They hadn't had enough time, though every couple in love probably thought the same thing. There was never enough time to satiate love's thirst. He stared at her with his frozen, milky eyes and Carly sobbed, a different tremor wracking her body, even if there were no salty tears.

The uncommon *slllllllu* of the sleigh sliding through the snow was all she heard. Carly's body finally calmed, her heartbeat slowing. She sniffed at the forest. Fuck the cold. Fuck Europe. She was returning to Australia, back to the desert. 'Straya. Hot and dry, water precious, the land sacred, and life even more so. Her lips felt dry, achey, and her tongue licked them slowly like a slug from a cave. The desert, the forest, flickered by like a stop-motion movie, smears of black against that eerie arctic light that wasn't quite light but wasn't quite dark. Smears of black on white toast.

"God, I would kill for some Vegemite," she said aloud, softly. She wondered if the reindeer heard her. She snorted. Of course he heard her; his ears flicked, and they were out of the forest now, a giant hill of white sands facing them, the tops of vibrant and healthy gum trees towering above. "Beautiful stuff," she said again to no one.

Running through that dreary and cold forest, a lifetime ago, giving everything to her flight, enough blood had finally coursed through her limbs and her core. Strong and always reliable, Carly's body had resumed its natural functions, taking care of itself and warming up. The reindeer started to really fly down the hill, kicking up sand that rubbed across Carly's face, and she was abruptly too warm. She felt like she had been on the run for hours, days, surely the sun was going to rise soon, maybe it was already nearby and the temperature of the land was rising. She felt it on her face, in her body, the sun was definitely approaching. Not the Australian sun, not the one that would brown her skin and golden her hair. An arctic Sun, but still a star.

There was the bizarre sensation she couldn't pinpoint that something wasn't as well as she wanted to believe. She was still hot. She opened the top of her jacket with stiff fingers, the heat of her body unimpeded by the quiet, stiff air. The kind of hot that made you sleepy, groggy, and lousy. But reason had been long-dispelled today, so she opened her jacket further.

The hill of sand ended, the reindeer rising, and suddenly Carly faced the sky. All her slow thoughts focused on how the weather so casually changed with its temperatures but the aurora never changed. It had been constant all night. "Beautiful stuff," she mumbled, not sure she said the words at all.

AINO

The two in the front didn't move nor offer help to Aino as they began traversing uphill. Most likely they couldn't even jump out in their thick layers if they wanted to; stopping meant they would slide back. So Aino and the reindeer continued pushing them up the low but far hill. Her muscles and lungs screamed at her. After an eon of toil, knowing if they didn't get to the top they would likely roll and return to the bottom, the reindeer pulled a little more of the weight and pressure left her hands. Aino looked up, the treeline only ten meters away, the bulk of the journey uphill complete.

Aino relaxed and the reindeer slowed, snorting air in great clouds, and he looked back to her as his driver. The threat of rolling down the hill was over. Sweat soaked her beanie and condensation was already turning cold on her hot skin. Pulling the scarf Carly had hastily wrapped around her, she wiped the water from her skin and heaved air. She turned back to look down the small valley she'd conquered. The opposite hill of snow was a wave of white foam in the night, laced with green. It was the most majestic panorama Aino ever witnessed in her short, unremarkable life.

"Shit!" Rocky exclaimed, jumping out of the sleigh.

"What? What!" Aino cried, her breath hoarse from the strenuous exercise.

He gestured to Carly, sitting still. Unmoving. Stiff.

Aino's strained breath nearly stopped, her lungs bursting to escape her chest with new dismay at what she would find if she just looked at Carly's face. Her shaky legs stepped wide and away, the reindeer watching her expectantly. Her stare stuck on the solid figure sitting erect in Aino's own spare black coat. "No, *nononononononono.*"

A final wide step revealed Carly's blanched face, a strange color that didn't belong on the living. Her eyes were closed, her hair frozen in rigid curly tendrils.

She was dead.

The top of her jacket lay open to bare, blanched skin, as if she was hot on the ride and trying to cool off. A cruel and twisted ending to hypothermia. Carly's brain, running haywire with slow blood and other organ failures, misregulated temperatures and tricked her into thinking herself hot.

Aino's knees buckled, her muscles already taxed from the hill. Despair sapped her will. Carly was decidedly the strong one among them, and the cold had bitten her too much. But her face was calm and there was something minutely relieving knowing she'd died serenely. Probably hallucinating, growing sleepy and tired until she just couldn't keep her eyes open. How everyone should hope to go.

A low snarl shuddered the valley. Aino felt it in her bones more than in her ears, like it reverberated in the earth. She turned just as the top layer of snow on the hill shuddered, molting like a mini avalanche. Rocky stepped forward, his features hypnotized.

"What is it?! Did you see it?" she asked.

His head shook. "I... it's big and looked... it had the face of a bear but it wasn't a bear."

Another grumble resounded through the air, Revontulet coursing in pulses too fast for the phenomena, too unnatural. Aino left Carly's frigid corpse. Across the valley, maybe two hundred meters at the opposite treeline, a figure cloaked in pitch padded onto the snow. Aino's body emptied of air, her gut again hollow.

Half the height of the trees behind it, the animal snuffled the ground with the distinct gait of a wolverine. The body was... vague. Black and indeterminate, but maybe a bear. A *fucking* mutant bear, a prehistoric mutation somehow surviving where no man lived. It grumbled, a distorted sound that carried and reached their hill, the string tugging Aino's heart again.

She was glued to the ground and her lungs, screaming for air, breathed again—breathing too fast. Her heart dropped through to her stomach. That monster would kill and consume them. It was the end of her and her time in the North. She was sure of it.

A heavy weight crunched the snow beside her feet, and Aino turned to Carly's rigid body, dumped from the sleigh and abandoned in the soft snow. She stared dumbfounded at Rocky as he smacked the wounded rump of the reindeer. It startled forward at his hit. "You coming?!" he yelled.

Clearly Rocky didn't care if she did or not, already assuming the position of rider. Recovering from her shock, Aino rushed the few feet onto the sleigh as it pulled away toward the treeline and onto another path made by her grandfather or ancestors. Aino looked back. In the distance, the goliath began *galloping* down the hill, snow spraying like waves at the beach.

"*Shushushushu*," she urged the reindeer, hoping it understood the urgency and would speed them through the dense forest. How had *it* gotten through the narrow tree lanes and still smelt them? Hell, forget why it tracked them, but rather *how*? They were upwind, their scent blowing away.

She exhaled when they were among the thicket, the reindeer racing faster with only two passengers, and Aino felt momentary shame for leaving Carly's corpse to be... whatever. Within a minute, they raced a well-worn trail, and Aino smiled for the first time that night when in the clear air of the trail, a line of faint smoke was high-lighted by the aurora.

"There!" she shouted above the rushing wind. "Just hold on!" She *shushushu*ed the reindeer, urging him faster. Smoke meant people. People meant a car, or a gun, or a phone, or *something*.

A minute passed and the smoke neared. The reindeer had undoubtedly traveled this way before. It was too well-marked; the old trees were purposefully planted in rows, creating a thin corridor, and she pondered how her grandfather had spent his time between her visits.

Finally, the trees ended at a small clearing. A log house sat in the cleared circle. Even in the dead of polar midnight, it was charming and quaint. But it was also dark and unlit. The reindeer slowed in the cleared yard like this was a normal stop on his mail route, and Aino and Rocky huffed hot clouds of air. Aino was stupefied. The house was cold, with no sign of life besides the thin trail of smoke from the small chimney. It was an old home; frozen carpet moss sat thick on the roof, and hand-cut logs were layered with the craftsmanship of another era. A small portal for a window had been made when glass wasn't available. More importantly, there was no car. No sign of modern civilization.

The hermit lived here.

The forest snarled, echoing through time, and Aino wanted to whimper. The beast had crossed the valley. Closing in, hasing them, pursuing them. She leaped from the sleigh, her tired legs pumping.

"Virtanen! Virtanen!" Aino hollered, running and banging on the door with her gloved fist. It was locked, so she stepped back, watching a small candle float through the darkness beyond the window.

The door wrenched open, a shotgun held up to her face. The old man she'd met briefly earlier had lost his skein of furs and exchanged them for a pair of fleece nightclothes. He was groggy and wary as he stepped from the house's dark innards and into the aurora light. His guarded expression changed to shock as he recognized her, and the gun lowered.

"Aino?"

Aino nearly cried. The flight from danger dogging her steps like a hellhound was too much, and she needed someone to take over. Her grandfather would know what to do; maybe this grandfatherly type was the same. The bones of the elderly were steeped in hard-earned wisdom. She blubbered through her lips in Finnish. "Mister Virtanen, please, something is chasing us. Something killed our guests. Do you have some way to get to the road? The reindeer won't be enough."

Deep rumbling surrounded the halo of trees, and the alarm on Virtanen's bearded face showed. He stepped from beneath the porch eave, examining the night sky, and swore before quickly grabbing both of her shoulders, angrily. His gun barrel dug into her arm.

"I told you not to go outside, foolish girl! Why couldn't you let it die!? Did you bleed in the lake?"

"What?"

"Did you bleed in the lake, girl!"

"No, what? No! I swear."

He gripped her upper arms tighter, and shook her to wring the truth out —a grandfather angry at a child for hurting themselves. Doing exactly as he'd told her not to.

"What about Mattias? Where is your father?"

"I... I don't know."

Dead.

He was dead. The knowledge certain in her bones.

She hadn't even thought about her father until now. She hadn't even considered him, all the delayed 'I love yous' now pointless and forever unspoken. Aino was a selfish creature, as all children begin, and as only some graduate from.

Virtanen's eyes widened as if she had said something completely different, confirming a suspicion. The three humans and one reindeer were startled by a sudden snarl. *Its* arrival was imminent–close enough Aino sensed it would suddenly lunge out of the canopy's darkness.

The hermit, her grandfather's friend-of-a-sort, licked his lips, eyes oscillating between Rocky, now dancing on the balls of his feet in anticipation of running or sprinting into the house, and Aino, staring with her doe eyes, begging for help.

Virtanen's voice adopted a sincere, paternal tone at odds with the franticness of Aino's nerves. "Look, it... it doesn't want to hurt you. It isn't... it doesn't want to hurt you. I can't explain and I can't help. But stop running. Just stop."

He backed away, stepping slowly towards his open door. Rocky came forward. "Wait, wait, what did he say? Hey! Aren't you gonna help us?"

Virtanen continued, his pitying stare locked with Aino's incredulous one, and was about to close the door on them.

"Well, at least... at least give us the gun!" Rocky stepped forward threateningly, but Virtanen raised the shotgun, and the American stopped in place, his gloved fist squeezing open and shut. The door closed and locked.

Rocky spun, bewildered and irate. "Well! What did he say? Is there some hidden car we ain't seeing? Does he know that *thing* is gonna tear his house apart?!"

Aino's body finally relented, her shoulders slumped, her eyes hooded. She was tired, exhausted, confused, groggy from exercise and the energy needed to stay alive in a place where only the vicious survived. She wasn't vicious, not even close. Her grandfather had been born with something absent in herself. He had a spirit that never tired of life and an enthusiasm for living here.

The beast grumbled outside the radial of light, its presence thick in the air. It was so close Aino heard distinct vocal cords rattle like plucked strings of a guitar.

"He said... to stop running. It wants me, he said." Tears mixed with snot and mourning for her dead father ran down her frosty face, dripping onto her jacket lapel. She studied the forest on her right, the pathway clear and distinct. An unknown light shone on it. No, it wasn't over yet. They'll take the reindeer, let him run the course he seemed to know.

Rocky mumbled, confused. "It wants you?"

She stepped toward the sleigh—and a monster attacked. Not a hard hoof, but still a bone, a fist full of knuckles covered in a glove struck her with uncanny accuracy at the back of her skull and she sank to her knees. Her vision swam, twos and threes of everything everywhere, and multiple Rockys ran ahead and away, jumping to be riders on the sleighs pulled by the reindeers, stealing her escape until they suddenly vanished.

Dazed, Aino tried standing, spinning in circles on shaky legs, her arms akimbo, reaching for an anchor to this world. But there was nothing, and in her spinning she caught sight of Virtanen. The crazy hermit who had told her to stay, spying on her from his shaded window, watching with grim anticipation. A low growl resonated through her body, every organ tugged on strings in the direction of the beast, and she spun to the trees. A pair of emerald stars blazed bright in the darkness of firs and pines. Rocky's punch throbbed the back of her head, forcing Aino to her knees and then flat to her back.

Green Revontulet swirled in her vision and burned bright and beautiful, except it was no longer the slender ribbons she knew. This was a blanket of green fire. A fiery quilt covered her land, filled with so much magnetism it crackled with electricity and raw power. She should scramble, on arms and legs and belly, do an army crawl. Do something.

A hoof stomped the ground beyond her feet—not aggressively but because its weight was immense.

Tears rolled down Aino's face. Feral breath snuffled around her, and a rotting smell invaded her senses. Not the rotting of trash, but rather the rotting of mulch, dead leaves cocooning new life beneath them. Life and death as one. A searching snout breathed quickly, susurrating the earth around her. Aino's head was so heavy, so tired and cold, she didn't even want to look up and thought it better to play dead. The snout nuzzled into the crook of her hand with a tickling wetness. Familiar and tender, it nosed itself deeper until her whole palm covered a soft nose, and Aino finally lifted her head.

And screamed.

All she could see was snout, so large, so close; it bared teeth, little daggers of bone, and it pressed hard into her belly. Hard enough to pin her, hard enough her internal organs were pushed aside. Cloth tore, Gorex ripped, and those teeth started snipping. Aino howled and cried. Her balled fist weakly pounded the snapping snout, the inflamed green stars meeting her stare right before the first little bite into her lower gut. Breath flew from Aino, a swarm of hot bees fighting to leave her body; her organs were on fire. Pain unmatched. It was eating her. Eating her essentials, digging deep, gouging a cavity inside her body, snuffing for her offals just like she had taken from the deer earlier that day. She was hollow again. A meal for the table.

She cried for help, reaching for the house with outstretched fingers. From his little window, Virtanen watched her being consumed, his face screwed up tight, sickened by its feast, sickened by the sight of her, and he dropped the curtain between them. She screamed shrilly, the last of her air given to the night, one final time before her head flopped to the ground once more. The fight left Aino.

Steam rose from the hole in her body, caught in heavenly luminescence. In her delirium, her bodily remains juddering with the bites, Aino watched her streaks of blood flow through the green fire. She thought how beautiful and terrible such a sight was right before you died. Her hands, no longer curled into fists, lifted and gently held the massive head burrowing into her, and she felt pine needles and soft fur beneath her fingers. She stroked it like a calf after birth. Comforting a baby feeding from a mother. She was feeding it, that's all. What a wonderfully horrid view. Aino hoped her soul wasn't stolen. She had covered her hair, after all.

THE SKY WAS BLACK GLASS. There was no moon. There were no stars. And there certainly wasn't any Revontulet. The trees had left and her hands were empty. The crater in her thorax was also gone. Aino stood naked and alone in a field of snow. But there was a musty, dank exhale reminiscent of red feathermoss and cut pine and reindeer fur and husky breath and biting river water and blood of salmon running through them. It was life and death and snow and sky. And then it was there again. The indescribable monster that was all the animals of the wild north and none of them. Only she and it, facing one another, pitch and snow surrounding them both. It neared and then somehow stood beside and inside and all around Aino, covering her like a blanket, like a mask, like a worm in the dirt. It was possessive and wanting. A possession. A host. The black glass of the cosmos shattered, exploded outward and inward, Revontulet burning everything. Burning faces of the sacred spirits. Burning the birch and pine that housed them. Burning the faces of her forefathers that housed *it*. It was black sky and green fire and blue water and their red blood melding all together and keeping separate.

All inside of Aino.

She sighed.

ROCKY

"*Huyah! Huyah!*" he shouted at the reindeer, spurring it like a stock horse. The only problem being Rocky was too far away for a good thrash, and the reindeer too stupid to realize they could both be eaten momentarily. The track curved away and he lost sight of the dilapidated shack and Aino stumbling like she should've been hauled to the drunk tank.

Guilt plagued his conscience for a hot moment before he remembered her words. It was after *her*. Fucking monstrosity probably smelled her native blood and had a liking for it. Like called to like and all that shit. Savages and savage animals. His heart panged for Regina. He recognized her holler as he took off, chasing after his escape. He had paused mid-stride but continued sprinting once the end of her scream was definite. Whatever happened to her Japanese whore, likely the other shriek he'd heard, he couldn't even pretend to be sorry.

The reindeer veered left down an unseen track, and Aino's howl ricocheted faintly. He unconsciously winced, each tremor, each rise and fall of her pained voice describing the way she was dying. Likely being eaten. Rocky's considerable weight shifted forward, and they left the protection of the trees. He immediately recognized the small valley of white walls they'd crossed earlier, except now the reindeer crossed at the very end of them.

Shit. They were returning to the lodge. The dumb animal was set on a course it wouldn't turn from, and he didn't know how to control the damn sleigh beyond stomping his foot down to brake. But no, maybe this was best; if they returned to the lodge, the animal could just run down the driveway instead of blundering through the forest. The driveway led to the road, and the road led to civilization. He had planned to just speed away in the car until it gave up, but the type of vehicle was of no concern. He could find a whip or long swatter and push the animal til it also died.

The sky above Rocky's head erupted, startling the reindeer and himself. It was terrifying, alien and unnatural, like a living thing, a behemoth searching for him and covering the land. The kinda shit to give you PTSD. He ducked his head, raising a protective forearm to cover his scalp while they crossed the open plain. Electric tendrils of green, enough to cover the immediate sky, enough to be seen for a hundred miles, a phenomenon the astronauts would notice. It fizzed and popped in his ears, barometric pressure or some shit changing, and he winced in pain.

After a moment of the reindeer's rhythmic hooves stomping snow, the sleigh's motion constant and steady, Rocky released his protective forearm and peeked out. They were nearly to the opposite treeline, and he examined the sky. A unique spire of red light faded back into the slender ribbons of chromatic green. He eyed it, wary. Enough of this fucking 'magic panoramas' for tonight. Surely the sky should be turning muddy gray soon? The sleigh dove into the trees, and the muffled hush of the forest painted in thick snow made Rocky cringe. His nerves, more shot to hell and tired than chewed twine, tingled. The quiet, *this* quiet, was sinister as shit. His only comfort was the reindeer snorting, another life filling the silence. Puffs of his breath dissipated by the time Rocky on the back of the sleigh passed them.

He scanned the surrounding wood, trusting the reindeer knew where he was headed. This area of the forest held trees tight and packed. The feathered-branch roof overhead was layered in thick, impenetrable snow, and the ground was much darker. No glowing snow or green aurora. It was quiet and then... not quiet. An indescribable hum filled his ears, similar to tinnitus or a sonic whistle for a dog. The reindeer slowed, and Rocky's eyes went to its shadowy backside as it stopped completely.

"Hey!" Rocky whispered. Tension in the frosted air abruptly raised the skin of his nape to gooseflesh. "*Huyah!*" he whispered without any other feeling but desperation. The reindeer didn't even look at him. Its antlers dimly glittered with ice, and it made a queer profile of indifference. "Fuckin animal," he muttered, his tone darker than coffin air.

He stepped off the sleigh's foothold, intent on giving the brute another smack on the rump, when halfway there, it all at once jumped into a run, legs pumping as if at the start of a race. Startled, Rocky turned to catch the handhold of the passing sleigh. His gloved palm grasped the bar, but the speed and his weight combined caused it to rip from his hand, wrenching him forward and splaying to the ground. He propped himself up on elbows, his molars grinding as the sleigh, already invisible in the dim light, deserted him.

Warm air plumed around his face, obscuring the umbra. Dammit, he should walk, no, run, just follow the tracks. Any fool could follow tracks in snow. Pushing to his feet, he wiped snow off his chest.

And stopped, his hand mid-brush.

A willowy, slender figure stood in the tracks of the narrow sled fifty feet away. She was naked, her birthday suit cloaked in shadows, her bare shoulders gleaming with faint light from above. Time stopped, and drifting snow paused in the air right before his eyes. Rocky inhaled sharply, a lump of coal stuck behind his tonsils. It wasn't for the sight of her free breasts, small and high with youth, nor the outline of lovely curves.

It was for the darkened patch in her flat stomach, black and dripping down her groin. Her heart-shaped face continued staring at the ground like a robot waiting to be switched on. Rocky sensed a presence behind her body, waiting to crawl over her slender shoulder, someone clinging to her back like an insidious leech, something hitching a ride. A passenger.

"Aino?" he spoke cautiously.

She didn't look up but stepped forward, and he reflexively stepped back like an opposing force.

Aino said something, the shadows of her lips moving, the sound lost on the insulated carpet of snow. "What?" he called. Panic laced his voice, a new sound, and she said it again, slowly walking. "Aino... are you... what is this? Stop this!" he commanded, invoking the timber of his voice that made Regina obey and office secretaries flinch.

Aino spoke again, still inaudibly, taking more steps forward. "Aino, I can't hear you but don't come... *STOP!*"

Her face lifted. She wore blood on her chin, and her mouth opened like an ingress to hell. Verdant fury burned inside her skull. She roared with a voice not hers and the very forest trembled.

"*OURS!*"

Shell-shocked, Rocky planted his feet defensively and she began running, rushing him, her body changing. He blinked twice, thrice. A colossal bear charged him, then an oversized wolverine, a behemoth reindeer with a mutated crown of antlers, a hunting wolf, a sprinting fox, little Aino. All translucent, all transmogrifying one step to the next, a dizzying, hypnotic display as several burning pairs of fire-green eyes marked him with furious rage. Aino was a mercurial ghost who couldn't decide on her body. She was all beasts and none of them.

She, *it*, was ten feet away when it occurred to Rocky to run. He turned his back on the girl only for antlers to impale his body in flight. Bone stabbed and a reindeer grunted, antlers poking through to the front of his jacket like little tents. His boots raised off the ground, taut pressure erupting his insides as the antlers lifted him to confront the sky.

Between the black tendrils of branches, the aurora sizzled the sky. The antlers inside him vanished, and his prostrate form fell fifteen feet to the ground, breaking ice and grit. A wolf covered him, matted fur black as midnight on a moonless night, pressing his shoulders down. Its breath huffed, the unique smell of fresh summer rain blowing on Rocky.

Its muzzle lowered to his face, his very bones petrified, muscles growing cold from sudden blood loss. It opened wide over his face and there was green fire and black stars and old voices, all humming a choir of unearthly hymns. Prayers for old, forgotten, and angry souls.

Rocky stared into the gullet, hypnotized, wondrous and holy knowledge dawning on him, even as the wolf began chewing off his face.

WILHOLM

Wilholm shook the Detective's hand, perfunctorily, but truly glad this was a parting shake. The older man nodded to Wilholm and then Aino, his gaze wandering down her simple long-sleeved shirt. It was 2 pm, twilight already dimming and lowering below minus five.

The Detective's SUV reversed up to the front step, and he addressed Aino one last time. "Call us or you can personally text me if you see any sign of him. Don't engage. Just keep your doors locked, yes? He will turn up soon when he gets hungry."

Instead of hugging her arms around herself for safety, the way Wilholm assumed a woman would when worried or frightened, Aino smiled warmly at the detective. "Of course, sir."

He mimicked her grin, maybe unconsciously, and then called, "Come on, old fellow," to the other man waiting in the main room, hanging back by the Christmas tree and staring into its lights with glazed eyes. Virtanen, the elder Wilholm had given a ride to three days ago with the Americans. Virtanen had made the trek to Aino's house all by himself earlier in the day. He'd worn an air of caution as he approached the detectives processing the crime scene outside and around the grounds. After listening to their story, he'd claimed that he too heard strange, indistinct sounds last night and thought he would check in with his only neighbor.

As was neighborly, he'd entered with them and remained quiet during the conversation with the police, but his thoughts seemed elsewhere as he heard the description of the suspect, a tall and broad American man with short black hair. Virtanen's eyes wandered to Aino on the couch every now and then, but besides that, he remained mute.

He now obeyed the detective and approached the door, standing in its frame and nodding to Aino. It was the first time he had spoken to her. "Okay, Aino?"

She smiled, easy and warm, confident in her answer. "I'm fine. Really."

His bushy eyebrows furrowed, and he gestured with a hooked thumb over his shoulder. "I'm just across the valley if you ever need me, or need to...talk and whatnot."

Again, Aino nodded happily. "Yes, I'm sure I can find your place, thank you."

Virtanen's eyes drifted down to where Wilholm's arm was wrapped around her shoulders. He looked as if he would say more, but his parted lips abruptly shut, and he walked down the steps to the waiting detectives. The car drove down the driveway, and the van holding the many bodies followed. It turned the bend. A moment later, the rumble of the engines was replaced by the whistle of a light breeze.

The wind rolled across the line of bordering trees, an invisible wave shuddering flakes from the humps of snow. Almost as if it called them, Wilholm's and Aino's heads followed the wave, right until it stopped opposite the house and their gazes lowered.

Dirty snow in long narrow shapes stained the ground before the porch. Wilholm's arm wrapped around Aino's neck, gently turning her away from the blood-soaked ground and into the house. A pointless gesture, probably. He certainly would never forget the sight of the women, mauled by wolves after being killed by the Texan; why would Aino?

But her arms came familiarly around his waist and he opened the door for them to walk in together. He released her and she him. He removed his jacket, watching her wander to the fireplace and sit on the love seat. She yawned wide and stretched her arms up in the air.

Wilholm smiled, no longer worried. After undergoing the medic's examination and relaying her story to the Detectives, Aino slept for sixteen hours. By hour twelve, Wilholm was worried. By hour fourteen, he had actually entered her room while the police still collected evidence and the fruitless manhunt was forming. He watched her deep breaths for a moment and then prodded her awake, afraid of a possible concussion. She woke groggily, telling him to let her sleep.

Now, a day later, she still behaved as if she had lived several lifetimes in the course of one night. Tired but calm. She stretched further across the arms of the chair, her body relaxing into the seat, molding into its curves. Relaxing. Something he hadn't thought her capable of after her ordeal.

He hung his hat on the hook, his gaze drifting to the translucent curtain to push it slightly aside with his finger.

"I've been sleeping in Matt... *his* room." He didn't know if they should start talking about her father yet. His floating body, such a clear silhouette under the ice of the lake, had been dredged up. "If that's okay, I'll stay in there tonight, just in case the American comes back, you know?"

Staring dreamily into the fire, she mumbled, "He's not coming back."

"Huh? He didn't say anything before he knocked you out, did he?"

Aino readjusted herself, unconcerned. "Wherever he is, he won't survive the cold."

Wilholm nodded and sat beside her, and she immediately lifted her legs across his lap and his heart picked up as he laid his hand on them comfortingly. Hearing the story pieced together by the detectives had been chilling. He'd listened and all he had wanted to do was help Aino, to hold her hand and wipe the tears he imagined she would shed. But she hadn't done anything like that so far. "You're probably right. Good riddance to someone who could do all that... savagery." He shuddered.

Aino groaned, "Ugghhh. Foreigners. Never again."

"Never again what?"

"Never again on our land. No hotels, no tours, no summer kayaking or shit like that."

He stiffened and smiled, examining her closer. Aino had changed. Grown more into herself somehow, like she had been wearing a suit all her life and finally matured into it.

"Our land?" he mocked.

She grinned, sinking further down, and her hand found his, entwining their fingers like winding cords of rope. "Well, you still need to take me out on that date. I believe it was meant to be *very* sexy."

Wilholm wasn't sure if it was the fire or he was blushing for the first time in his life, but he was suddenly hot, and his grin moved into the corner of his mouth. Before he could reply, a weight scraped the wood porch and he flinched, shifting her legs off to look over his shoulder and the front door. The sound repeated, and he rose to his feet and crossed to the window.

In the porch light, a branch had been pushed by the wind and gotten stuck against the porch's post. A gust blew and the small branch *thudded* against the wood again. Aino's hand rubbed his shoulder, joining him at the window.

"Supposed to be a beautiful night. Strong Revontulet," he commented.

Her fingers kneaded his shoulder, traveling up to his hairline, and threading through his hair. It tingled in his groin. "Should we rug up and get ready to watch?"

She chuckled and ducked her head to try and see past the porch's roof. He looked aside to her and for an instant, his breath stuck. Her eyes, gazing upward, were bright green. The irises, the whites, the entire orb was that special neon green of the Revontulet. Like a nebula lived in her head. He quickly followed her stare, thinking they reflected an early aurora.

But the sky was clear, the early rising moon illuminating across the sky.

"Aino?" he whispered.

She blinked and turned to him, and he exhaled at her normal hazel eyes. Beautiful hazel eyes.

"The igloos? It could take your mind off of... It should be beautiful."

"Yes, beautiful," she smiled.

THE END

Acknowledgments

There are many people who help in the process of bringing a story onto paper. Thank you to my loving family, who are supportive in every way to the writing process. Thank you to my husband who just nods and says 'of course!' when his maniac wife proclaims she needs a vacation and is going to the Arctic circle in a few weeks. Thank you to my friend, Jessica, who happily agreed to come on a once in a lifetime trip to Lapland and went far too-excitingly fast on the dog sled. Thank you to my beta-friends, Steve Neal, Camilla Brox, Mark Robinson, and Stephen Howard. Thank you to the wonderful blurb authors I call friends but aspire to call colleagues, Tim McGregor, Kenzie Jennings, and Laurel Hightower. Thank you to Elizabeth Rands who read a very odd query letter and took to it enough to read further (and then some). Thank you to Teemu Puukka who has been patient and kind and understanding with creating a wonderful, authentic cover (with lots of easter eggs!). Thank you to readers who have bought this labor of love and were inspired to buy my other writings. Thank you to Jill Giardi for first giving me hope. Thank you to my Wednesday night writing crew who provide emotional support whenever needed. Thank you to podcasters, reviewers, publishers, booksellers, and all the many others who help spread a book's message and tell a friend about it. You're all wonderful. Thank you for reading, hope you had fun.

ABOUT THE AUTHOR

Rowan Hill is an Australian/American author who has lived a little bit of everywhere. She primarily writes horror in isolated environments and feels everything is better with a creature feature. Self described as an 80s child, Rowan loves a good synth soundtrack and her hobbies include hiking mountains and traveling to far off places that she probably shouldn't. She can be found on social media as writerrowanhill or her website of the same name.

ALSO BY ROWAN HILL

In the Arctic Sun

ABOUT THE PUBLISHER

Bayou Wolf Press is an independent publisher of quality fiction. If you enjoyed this book and would like to support us, the best thing you can do is leave a review on Amazon, Goodreads, or wherever you review books. If you'd like to learn more about our press, sign up for our newsletter, and stay informed on upcoming books, please visit www.bayouwolf.com .

www.ingramcontent.com/pod-product-compliance
Lightning Source LLC
Chambersburg PA
CBHW060453300726
48975CB00008B/2494